Advance Praise for Island Gambit

In her newest journey to Papua New Guinea, Bridges shifts effortlessly between voices as she describes what the Christian life looks like from different perspectives. The book explores the allure of evil, the pursuit of purpose, and the possibility for personal transformation while delivering readers a fast-paced adventure.

Sabrina Zirkle
Corporate writer, English and comparative literature student

Island Gambit transports the reader to the ruggedly beautiful isle of New Guinea, where the teens of a missionary family encounter mystery, romance, friendship, danger and a natural disaster. Bridges artfully weaves folklore, colorful traditions and native language into an alluring story that, at its core, serves as a powerful reminder that each of us has a unique ability to help fix this broken world.

Susan Miura
Author of Healer

Vivid descriptions of the native locale immerse you in a new world while simultaneously grounding us in the struggles we often face in our Christian walk. Add in a perilous natural event along with a human threat of danger and *Island Gambit* offers a compelling read.

Christie Kern
Author

Felicia Bridges

Island Gambit

International Mission Force Series
Book IV

Felicia Bridges

Adventures Inspiring Action Publishers
Raleigh, NC 27616

Dedication

This book is dedicated to the women of Papua New Guinea who have been victims of Sorcery Accusation Related Violence and to the heroes working to save them.

Acknowledgements

Island Gambit has been the most arduous writing adventure yet. From venturing out from the security of being traditionally published, to pressing on through a pandemic, to learning the ropes of self-publishing, the last several years have required clinging to the hem of the Lord's robe.

Thank you to John and Lena Allen and Anton Lutz who served as my virtual tour guides, introducing me to their beloved PNG. As long-term missionaries, they shared so much of their experiences, both the beautiful and the tragic, to help me capture it all for my readers. Special thanks to Anton for his generosity in sharing his beautiful photography so that I could share his photos with my readers on my website. Thanks, too, for introducing me to your PNG friends who read and affirmed that I had represented the realities of life in Papua New Guinea well.

Thank you to Mary Beth Dahl for your eagle-eyed edits. What a blessing you are to me!

Thanks to my many, many prayer warriors – the Light Brigade, Sisters by Grace, Recharged, and our Summit Church small group. When you pray, God moves mountains and He definitely did in this case.

Thanks to my faithful readers – the ones who kept asking, "When is the next book coming out?" You kept me going when I might have given up.

Thank you to my adult children and their families for their encouragement and belief in me, and to my mom, always my biggest fan.

As always, thank you to my husband Randy for continuing to support and encourage me and for

seeing my writing as the ministry that it is.
Finally and above all, thank you, Jesus, for saving me,
for guiding me, for inspiring me, for loving me.

Dear reader,

Thank you for joining me on the fourth adventure in the International Mission Force journey. In response to homeschooling families, I'm including resources to promote understanding of the historical background and culture of Papua New Guinea, and I've added similar resources for the first three volumes in the series on the International Mission Force website. I've also included a glossary, including some common Tok Pisin words and discussion questions at the end of the book. Links to additional resources can be found at
www.InternationalMissionForce.com.

New Guinea is the second largest island in the world, after Greenland. The eastern half of the island is the independent nation of Papua New Guinea, while Indonesia governs the western half, composed of the provinces of Papua and West Papua. It is the most linguistically diverse place on earth, with eight hundred sixty languages in Papua New Guinea and its associated islands and at least as many distinct tribes.

There are a variety of missionary organizations which serve these often-isolated tribes, and I've incorporated features of different organizations, locations, tribes, and customs to capture the beautiful diversity of this culture. As a result, specific settings outside of Port Moresby reflect a compilation of details from around the country rather than the specific characteristics of one location, tribe, or organization.

With so many people groups, some of whom were unaware of the existence of any human beings outside their tribe until as little as sixty years ago, there is also an array of diverse folklore, rather than shared folklore common to all Papuans. Therefore, rather than selecting a single folktale, as in previous volumes of the International Mission Force, I've collected various tales from the region and included them as an appendix. In retelling them, I've sought to capture the unique and charming style of storytelling prevalent in Melanesia. This may include the story ending abruptly, without a clear moral to the story or a conclusion that is apparent to the reader. These stories provide a glimpse into Melanesian culture. You can also find links to the sources for these and other legends on the **International Mission Force** website.

As always, thank you for joining me on this adventure!

Felicia Bridges

CHAPTER ONE

Wara, Eastern Highlands Province, Papua New Guinea

The village glasman silenced the drums with a wave of his hand and shook a crooked, bony finger in Moia's face. His voice rang out.

"Sanguma!"

The angry crowd froze in horror around her.

Moia's legs trembled. She'd heard the charge before. In fact, nearly every year, the tribe's medicine man had a new revelation, revealing a new accusation. A trial was unnecessary. The glasman knew. The people believed.

The mob turned toward her, their eyes following their leader's gesture. She shifted her baby girl, Isa, to her other hip and grabbed her son's hand. Her oldest, Laila, reached for her, but the crowd swarmed around them until Moia couldn't see her. Brutal hands pulled Rayz's hand from her grip and ripped Isa from her arms.

The bare, black chests of warriors, painted with red, yellow, and white and decorated with brightly colored feathers, reminded her of all the moments of grief which filled her life. The pungent smoke of the ceremonial fire stung her nostrils. They mourned today for her husband, a leader in their tribe. Her heart ached at the memory, but she had no time now to grieve. Her people pressed closer as she cowered before her accuser.

Her husband's death provided all the proof

needed for the glasman to accuse her of being a sorceress, a sanguma, and pass a death sentence which the tribe would dutifully carry out.

She searched the painted faces for a gap, a familiar smile, a glimmer of hope.

There—her little sister!

But that beloved face, the one she'd kissed and doted on, twisted into a vicious grimace. Her gaze darted to the right of the girl.

Her father!

But he, too, bore the mask of hatred she had seen before.

She had participated in previous rituals, had believed the glasman when he cast the lot. She had trusted he knew best for the tribe. He alone could identify the witches known as sanguma, who consumed a person's innards and replaced them with ash, killing them slowly as the victim coughed up blood and eventually expired.

But he cared nothing about her innocence. Her mind rebelled against the accusations. She'd watched her husband grow sick and had cared for him the best she could.

A young man seized her wrists and wrapped an emerald vine of liana around them. Despite the paint he wore, she recognized him as Kuni, her husband's brother. He dragged her to a nearby casuarina tree and secured her to the rough, splintery trunk. The texture scraped at her bare chest and belly, leaving angry red streaks in her dark flesh. The sound of Isa wailing tore at her heart.

"It's not true! I'm not a sanguma!" She cried out to her sister and her father. "Help me! Tell them it's not me."

But tradition ruled more powerfully than blood,

and she knew from experience that her words were no more convincing than those who had cried out as they endured this fate before. The result would be the same. They no longer saw her as sister, daughter, or friend, but as a demon who had killed her own husband and would kill them all if they didn't purge her from their midst.

Fear, superstition, and self-preservation fueled their cruelty.

Her heart raced as the first blow fell across her back, and memories which tormented her dreams became a prophecy of what her future held. They would torture her for days, trying to force her to name others who participated in her presumed witchcraft until her suffering finally ended in a blazing fire.

The second blow brought searing pain. The forest blurred and faded. Her cheek rested on the rough casuarina, oblivious to the pain of its splinters piercing her skin. Raised voices surrounded her, but even those seemed muted and far away.

A gentle one silenced the others. Her anguished mind couldn't comprehend the words. She waited, steeling herself against more pain. Her eyelids drooped, and she welcomed the darkness.

But the next blow never came.

Three months later, outside the Haedi Outpost, Eastern Highlands Province, Papua New Guinea

Toby raced the coming darkness back to the fenced campus of the language institute. A chill bolted down his spine at the thought of being caught outside alone after dark. The small community of missionaries had good reasons for the gates which guarded them.

He stumbled down the muddy path, his size thirteen sneakers thumping like tribal drums as he quickened his pace. Long shadows chased him as he tried to dodge a puddle but landed with a splash, drenching his shoes in thick, dark mud.

He'd spent the afternoon delivering medicine to Miss Maryann, a missionary in Wara. The trip required a two-hour hike from his home across two rickety suspension bridges which spanned the Hegigio River and the deep gorge it had cut through the mountains. Miss Maryann, the seventy-something-year-old former Army nurse, lived in a small, wood-planked, tin-roofed cabin which doubled as a health clinic for the villagers. With only a tiny solar-powered cooler for the meds she kept on hand, Toby and his family made weekly trips to restock her supplies. She was pretty tough for a little old lady. She never complained about living without running water or electricity and being isolated by the rugged terrain.

He'd made the trip a dozen times with his father or brother, but never by himself. His parents would be furious with him for going alone. And even more so if they knew about him wandering off the trail and about his gruesome discovery.

He rounded the corner as the guard began closing the gate.

Pushing himself to speed up, he lifted his knees higher, but it didn't seem to make much difference. His arms swung at his sides, but not smoothly like Brandon, his athletic older brother. Instead, they pumped awkwardly, unable to match the rhythm of his legs well. His glasses bounced on his nose, and sweat blurred the lenses.

"Wait! Wait a minute." He called out, and Mr. Dan, the security guard, looked his way and frowned.

"Thanks, Mr. Dan," he called over his shoulder breathlessly as he slipped through the gate and slowed to a jog.

"It's almost dark, Toby." Mr. Dan plastered a scowl over his habitual smile.

"Sorry, Miss Maryann was telling me stories about life in the village."

"How old are you now?" Hands on his broad hips, the belt of his uniform almost hidden by his belly, the guard persisted.

Toby knew where this conversation was headed but answered anyway.

"Fourteen."

"Old enough to know better than to lollygag after dark. I'm sure your folks warned you about the bands of rascals looking for an easy mark. There have been several robberies—" Mr. Dan stopped his lecture and looked back through the gate, expecting someone else. He called out as Toby kept moving, "Where's your brother?"

Toby glanced back to see the older man shaking his head again and muttering about kids and danger. The friendly, pot-bellied guard treated all the kids in the community like they were his own, though he'd never married. He worked for the company which provided security for the satellite linguistics center. Most of the security staff were locals, but Dan frequently covered the gate at closing time, determined to ensure he'd safely tucked everyone in.

Toby bounded down the narrow, unpaved road to the small house on stilts which he'd called home for half his life. The linguistics center stood in a low-lying valley near the river, and they built their homes about four feet off the ground to protect them from occasional flooding. Sparse broad-leafed evergreen trees dotted the space between the houses, offering a little shade on the rare hot day. Most of the year, they enjoyed ideal tropical weather.

He paused to catch his breath and greet the family pet, a New Guinea Singing Dog they'd found abandoned as a pup. Bublé had earned his name with his warbling howl. Toby rubbed the pooch's tawny ears, and Bublé licked his fingers and rewarded him with a few melodious notes.

"Just a minute, Bublé." Toby's words came in short spurts in between deep breaths. "I'll get your dinner soon." Bublé crooned a response.

Taking the steps two at a time, Toby threw open the door and trailed muddy footprints across the kitchen.

"I almost didn't make it back in time." He dropped with a thud into a sturdy chair at the kitchen table. His mother stood in front of the small stove and stirred the concoction of sweet potatoes and other vegetables. His heart pounded. What would she say about him almost getting caught outside the gate when it closed for the night?

Without looking up, she shrugged. "Actually,

you're right on time. Dinner should be ready in five minutes."

She finally glanced his way, and her eyes widened at the mess he'd made. "Tobias, you know you're supposed to take off your shoes at the door. What were you thinking?"

She rinsed off a washcloth and tossed it to him. "Please clean up your mess. And feed Bublé. And then call your brother and your sisters to dinner." Her tone sounded uncharacteristically harsh, and a deep line creased her brow. He recognized the signs they'd had a sad ending for a patient at the clinic where she served as a nurse.

"No, I meant . . . Never mind." He pushed himself up from the table, causing it to groan under the pressure. Backtracking to the door, he slipped off his shoes and lined them up next to the others outside the door. He dropped to his knees and swiped away the mud, his lips pressed tight against a tidal wave of resentment. When he had cleaned the floor, he tossed the rag into a basket of dirty laundry. His sister Amy would wash it all by hand and hang it on the lines in the yard tomorrow.

Grabbing a scoop of the mix of table scraps, kaukau, and rice they fed the dog, he dumped it in the bowl on the porch. Bublé ran to greet him the moment he called. At least his dog listened to him.

Well, when Toby had food, he listened.

Toby buried his face in the short, soft fur and pressed his eyes shut tight against the sting of tears before reluctantly pulling away.

Ducking his head, he pushed the bridge of his glasses up his nose with an index finger and clomped inside and down the hallway. "Brandon-Amy-Ruth! Dinner time!" His voice filled the narrow space and shook the thin walls. Amy and Ruth emerged from their room and crowded into the single bathroom to wash their hands.

Toby leaned into the open doorway of the room he shared with his older brother. Brandon sat in the middle of the bottom bunk bed, his back against the wall and knees folded almost double in front of him, as he rocked the air drums to the music oozing out of his headphones.

"Brandon!" Toby yelled louder, but his brother ignored him. He jumped in front of the seventeen-year-old's view and waved his arms wildly until Brandon lifted the headset from one ear, allowing the deep thump of the bass to fill the room. Toby's heart felt every thump just as he had in the village.

"It's dinnertime. I've been calling you, and you keep ignoring me." An acidy taste burned his throat. Ignored. Invisible. The story of his life. His face felt hot and not from his mad dash back to the institute.

"I'll be there in a minute, little dude."

Little dude. The nickname lingered from years before and made him feel like a powerless child looking up to his perfect big brother once again.

Truthfully, he'd grown taller than Brandon and outweighed him by thirty pounds. Some days he wanted to show his older brother what this "little dude" could do.

He blamed Brandon for being on the trail alone today. If anything had happened to him, that would have been Brandon's fault, too. He pushed away any thought of his own responsibility for his choices.

Toby pressed his lips together and turned to leave the room.

The girls rushed by as he emerged, knocking him off balance. He fell against the wall with a whomp that threatened to knock the picture off the wall. He steadied the picture, but then clenched a fist and struck the wall hard enough to hurt.

"Really?" he muttered through gritted teeth. Stepping into the tiny bathroom jammed with a small sink, toilet, and shower, he gripped the sink. He imagined tearing the sink from the wall and crashing it on the floor. The thought teased him with a sense of satisfaction, but he drew in a deep breath and slowly released it. Venting his anger would only lead to trouble.

Instead, he washed his hands.

He reached for a towel and caught sight of his reflection in the mirror. Beet red cheeks, spotted with freckles, framed his grimace. His fair skin always broadcast his emotions. Splashing the tepid water on his cheeks, he set his glasses aside and toweled his face dry. He let his breath out slowly again, this time exhaling into the coarse towel. One more glance in the mirror to be sure his cheeks had returned to a normal shade of pink, and then he put his glasses on and joined his family in the kitchen.

His father appeared in the doorway of his office, which doubled as his parents' bedroom, and rubbed his eyes from a long day at the computer. Pressing his hands into his back and stretching as he yawned, he then crossed the living room in a few long strides. He caught Toby's mom for a quick kiss before he took the large pot of kaukau from her hands and carried it to the table.

"Toby, I asked you to call your brother." His mother sat down as she cast a glance of reprimand in his direction.

"Are you kidding me?" He threw his hands in the air. "I did. He won't listen to me! Nobody in this family ever listens to me."

"Young man! You need to apologize to your mother." His father's voice commanded obedience, though for a split-second Toby contemplated defiance.

Brandon appeared before he could respond. "What's the problem, little dude? I'm here now. Don't get so uptight." He popped Toby on the shoulder with a jab.

Toby's frustration simmered, and he murmured an apology he definitely didn't feel.

He almost hadn't made it back home before dark, and he'd made the entire trek alone. But what did they care? He could have fallen off that crazy bridge or been bitten by a poisonous snake. He could have even been killed and swallowed whole by a python, like in the video he'd seen online. Maybe they would care if they had to cut him out of a giant snake. But if he mentioned the video, Mom would say he spent too much time online and cut his screen time.

His father prayed over the food. As they served their portions and passed the pot of kaukau, his father asked, "Did you boys have any trouble getting the medicine to Miss Maryann? I worry about her living alone in the village, but she insists she knows what she's doing, and they need her. Without her clinic, they'd still be depending on the glasman for medical care."

Toby had thought for a moment his father might be worried about him, but his dad only worried about the little old lady and her medicine. Toby loved Miss Maryann. She'd been a surrogate grandma since his own lived on the other side of the planet, but in the moment, jealousy and bitterness soured his stomach.

He glanced across the table at Brandon and

locked eyes. Would Brandon confess to tricking Toby into going alone?

Brandon jumped in before Toby could answer. "Dad, I was going to go with Toby, but he took off before I finished my homework. By the time I realized he was gone, it was too late for me to catch up with him."

His father's gaze turned toward Toby, whose mouth gaped at his brother's distortion of the facts.

"That's not what happened, and you know it, Brandon. You said to go ahead, and you would catch up, but you never did." He felt the color return to his face, and his eyes stung with salty tears threatening to escape. Angry as much at his own anxieties as his brother's betrayal, he slammed his fist on the table and the glasses jumped, sloshing water but not tipping over.

"I made it to Wara fine without you." He lifted his chin for a moment in defiance. Then the energy driven by his anger faded as he remembered how close he'd come to being stuck outside the gate in the dark. He sank into his seat. "But we talked for longer than I thought. I almost didn't make it back before Mr. Dan closed the gate." His voice rose in timbre from an angry snarl to a higher-pitched whine.

His father stopped chewing and made eye contact with him.

"Toby, we've talked about how important it is to be home before dark." His dad's calm, but firm voice chastened Toby as he flashed a frown at Brandon. "And about traveling alone. We'll talk later about your responsibility."

Well, what do you know? Maybe his dad saw through his brother's deception, after all. But Toby poured out his rehearsed excuse for being late anyway.

"Miss Maryann told me about everything that has been happening in the village. She said the glasman has been discouraging people from reading the Bibles she gave out. He tells them if they follow a white god, their own gods will be angry and won't send rain for them to grow their kaukau. And a few months ago, she heard he had accused a woman in the village of witchcraft after her husband died. They were going to hurt her, but Miss Maryann helped her escape."

His father's brow wrinkled, and he glanced at Toby's mother. "Moia." Their eyes exchanged a private message.

The crease between his mother's eyes returned, and she shook her head. "I'm glad we could help her save Moia, but what if this isn't over? Maryann stood up to a leader in their tribe. Who knows what he might do? I know she likes to chat, and she misses having folks to talk with, but she knows better than to keep Toby too late. And to fuel his imagination with frightening stories." She turned to Toby. "And you know better than to go alone."

Toby hung his head. It wasn't really Miss Maryann's fault. Because of his fascination with the tribe she lived among, he'd pressed her to tell him more.

At an age when most would opt for shuffleboard and card games, she chose to learn a challenging new language so she could provide medical care to people in need. She'd been serving around the world her whole life on battlefields and in poverty-stricken emergency rooms. She had a million stories to tell.

But even after listening to her stories, he'd have made it in plenty of time if he'd come straight home. Instead, he'd stopped to take a leak in the woods which had led to his big discovery. But he wasn't about to tell them about venturing off the trail or about what he found. Not until he knew what it meant.

His dad was right. He knew better than to go alone, but Brandon had instigated it by saying he didn't have time to babysit his little brother.

His mother's voice broke into his thoughts. "I don't like the idea of Toby traveling such a long distance. Maybe you and Brandon should make the trip from now on."

"I'm not a little kid. I walk to the village at Haedi all the time. I can walk to Wara!" Toby cringed at the volume of his own outburst. All eyes at the table were on him again, and suddenly he wanted to crawl under the table. He pushed the food around on his plate and murmured an apology for yelling. Glancing up at his mother, he caught the look she gave his dad, her hand raised as if to keep him in his seat.

Her calm voice soothed Toby's frayed temperament. "Toby, I know you aren't a little kid. But walking to Wara alone isn't safe; the trail is full of all sorts of dangers. Not just bands of rascals lurking after dark, but poisonous snakes as well. The path itself is dangerous...." Her voice trailed off. His imagination conjured other dangers even more frightening than snakes. He'd read stories of cannibalism in the not-so-distant past.

When Miss Maryann had told him about rescuing the woman from the glasman, it sent a chill up his spine. She had intervened just in time and sent the victim and her children to Haedi for refuge. Toby didn't really believe the glasman had any magical powers, but he'd heard his parents talk about what happened if he accused someone of witchcraft. The thought made his stomach twist and his face felt cold.

"I know. I'm sorry. Next time I'll be more careful, and I won't go alone."

His parents and siblings ate in silence for several tense moments until his mom said, "I'll give you one more chance, but if you go off by yourself again, it will be the last time."

His brother let out an almost silent sigh, obvious only to Toby. Great, so Brandon would make the next trip especially miserable as payback for having to accompany his little brother.

Toby finished his meal, ignoring the conversation around the table about what they had done today. He wasn't sulking. Talking about the same old happenings at the institute bored him. He replayed the stories he'd heard from Miss Maryann and his discovery in the woods over and over. At least until his father mentioned the air strip.

"I need to take the Mule to the airstrip in the morning. John is bringing us a barrel of gasoline. I'll be leaving as soon as the sun is up."

The four kids erupted in a chorus of reasons each of them should go with him. Riding in the Kawasaki Mule 4X4 to the airstrip at Balus and watching the single-engine Kodiak bush plane land provided a thrill Toby and his siblings frequently squabbled over. The bench seat allowed room for just three people to squeeze in and still have room for the supplies to be piled on the back.

His dad raised a hand to silence the pleading voices. "Sorry, girls. I'll have to take Toby and Brandon this time to help me get the drum onto the Mule."

The girls' faces fell, but they didn't complain.

"How about if we make taro pudding and wild

berry jam while they're gone?" Mom tried to placate them with a day of making sweets, and Ruth smiled and nodded, but Amy frowned.

"I want to help with something which actually matters. Not just make pudding." She crossed her arms. "I'm seventeen. Girls my age are rescuing victims of human trafficking, working to train deaf believers to share their faith, or rescuing their own parents from prison. Even here, folks come halfway around the world to serve, and they're out helping build or paint or do all sorts of work around this community or even in the villages. Even Brandon and Toby are helping by taking supplies to Miss Maryann. All while I'm stuck doing homework or chores around the house."

Toby smirked at his sister's complaint, grateful to have the attention turn to someone else's problems and pleasantly surprised to be an object of her envy.

"Your work is to finish studying and to help our family. We all have a role to play, Amy. And wanting to do the work God has given others is envy, just as much as wanting someone else's house, or clothes, or money." Their father responded with his usual calm logic. He raised his eyebrows and waited patiently for her mumbled agreement.

His mom nodded, and added, "But I know something you could do. We helped Maryann relocate Moia and her three children to Haedi, and her daughter is about your age. It's hard to imagine the trauma she witnessed. I'm sure the transition hasn't been easy, and she could use a friend?" Her mother's voice turned the statement into a question.

Amy shrugged. "Okay, I guess that's something."

"It's more than just 'something.' Helping someone who has suffered so much is one of the most important ways we can serve."

Amy nodded.

With the pot of kaukau emptied, Toby's mom turned back to him and decreed, "Speaking of each of us having a role to play, it's your night for dishes, Toby."

Of course it was.

Amy sat at the small side table and opened the solar powered laptop she shared with her siblings. She clicked on the International Mission Force website, eager to read about the work other teenagers around the globe were doing. Several new posts had come in, and she scanned through the adventures her online friends had shared. Political coups, drug kingpins, gang violence. It seemed like they were constantly caught in a race for their life, with God rescuing them from all sorts of trouble. She didn't wish for something terrible to happen, but couldn't she do something more exciting than laundry, homework, and dishes?

She lived in the most exotic place of all, but monotonous routines filled her days. While her father translated the Bible into one of the many tribal languages and her mother cared for patients in the local clinic, she spent her days listening to teachers, doing homework, then coming home to chores.

They had come to Papua New Guinea when she was ten, and it had been so thrilling and a little scary back then. But now, life on the tropical island seemed abysmally normal. Sure, she had to hang clothes out to dry rather than put them in a dryer like they'd had at home. She had to limit her online time because the computer had a limited charge, depending on how sunny the day was, and she had to share it with her siblings rather than having a device of her own. She also spent more time walking instead of riding in a car and doing chores rather than playing games or watching TV. But it had all become so boring.

None of it made a difference. Nothing she did mattered. The pastor would preach again on Sunday about the importance of serving God, but housework didn't feel very spiritual.

She sighed. Her mom had suggested she could help by being a friend to Moia's daughter, Laila. She could do that. But she wanted to do something big. She wanted to feel useful and effective, to contribute in meaningful ways to the work here. She wanted to help the people they had come to the island to serve. If God had a purpose for her life, as her parents and the pastor said so often, she wanted to find it.

Brandon tossed a soft foam ball at the back of her head. "My turn, Ay-by."

She scooped it up and tossed it back at him but missed by a mile. "I told you not to call me that."

He'd coined the nickname when she was born less than a year behind him. He'd been too little to say "Amy," or maybe his parents calling her "Amy" sometimes and calling her "baby" at other times confused him. The nickname never failed to irritate her. She flipped her short blond hair back and stuck out her tongue before relinquishing the laptop. She retreated to the minimal privacy of the room she shared with Ruth.

Grabbing her book from the dresser, she plopped down on her bed, leaning against the wall as she drew her knees up in front of her. She used her thighs as a bookrest as she flipped open to where she had left off reading about the various ancient creation stories.

The region known as Melanesia seemed to have as many myths as it did islands. Each island had developed a culture and a history all its own. And the island they lived on, divided between Indonesia and Papua New Guinea, had hundreds of legends and rituals for its countless different tribes and languages.

Many of the legends bore a stark resemblance to biblical accounts of the creation of man or the flood during Noah's time, or at the least, included some elements in common. None of the stories depicted the origin of the earth, but various stories told about the beginnings of mankind. The words carried her out of her bedroom and into the mysterious world of long ago.

Toby lay on the top bunk in the dark, staring at the object he'd picked up along the trail on his way home. His eyes adjusted to the faint light of stars filtering through the window, and he examined the smooth finish and knobby ends. He leaned over the edge of the bed and watched Brandon to be sure he was asleep before pulling the small flashlight, his journal, and a pencil from under his mattress. With the dim flashlight tucked under his chin, he sketched the outline of the piece from several angles. He turned the small object over and over in his hands, holding it up against the index finger of his left hand. It was slightly shorter than the length between his knuckle and first joint. A proximal phalanx bone. He'd looked it up online when he should have been doing homework. He held the bone up to his sketch and filled in shading to mimic the slightly brownish discoloration.

He had only noticed the tiny bone because he ventured off the path near the village, so he didn't dare tell his parents or his brother. If getting home late or traveling to the village alone caused all the tension they'd had at dinner, leaving the trail and wandering into the woods would really make them crazy. And they'd sure never let him go to Wara again.

His imagination conjured the finger of a native child, perhaps left behind by a wild animal, like Toby might leave the crust of bread from his sandwich on the plate. Or maybe the child got lost from his or her family and starved in the jungle, his bones scattered by dogs or wild pigs over decades since his death. Perhaps a witch had captured the child and sacrificed him in an ancient ritual. Toby knew battles sometimes erupted between neighboring tribes and had heard some practiced cannibalism in the most remote villages. His dad said they were rumors and nonsense . . . but still . . ..

He turned the bone over again in his palm, and a shiver of part fear, part intrigue, slithered up his spine. Curiosity and fantasy teased him with a million different pictures, and his compulsion to explore further grew.

The familiar sound of his brother's deep breathing on the bunk below lulled him. He couldn't tell anyone, and certainly not Brandon, who would tell their dad for sure. But the next time he carried medicine to Miss Maryann, he'd leave the village early enough to allow more time to explore on the way home. Somehow, he would have to ditch his brother first.

CHAPTER TWO

Motukea Island Dockyard, Port Moresby, Papua New Guinea, one month later

After almost a month onboard the MSC Katie, Slane fought the urge to kiss the ground when they docked at Motukea to unload the cargo of heavy equipment and machinery.

Working as an ordinary seaman had provided the perfect escape after the remnants of Gerardo's cartel had tracked him to the alleys of Iquiqui.

Life had finally been going his way until he'd made the mistake of befriending that sniveling bartender with the red nose and glassy eyes. He should have recognized the symptoms of the scrawny addict. His experience with the cartel should have warned him Juan's addiction would drive the man to betray his own mother for a fix.

His so-called friend had asked him to carry out the garbage at the end of a shift, and Gerardo's henchmen had been waiting for him. Only quick thinking and a boatload of unbelievable luck had allowed him to escape alive.

After such a close call, he'd stuck with jobs which required no identification and which led him farther and farther from his past in Bolivia. He'd worked his way up the Pacific coast of South America, moving from one town to the next. When he'd reached Callao, Peru and seen the huge container ships docked at the port, he seized a glimmer of hope he might escape the dying grasp of the cartel forever.

He'd spent four weeks learning the duties of an

ordinary seaman from Joaquin, an able seaman Slane had apprenticed with since he boarded in Callao. As the tugboats pressed the MSC Katie close to the dock, Slane and Joaquin passed the heavy mooring lines down to the shore men.

Once they secured the ship, the captain gave them the afternoon off and thirty kina apiece to buy lunch. Slane stuffed the money into the pocket of his frayed jeans. He followed his mentor down the walkway to the cement dock as Joaquin boasted of knowing the best coffee spot in Port Moresby.

Slane's knees quaked as he regained his balance on land after becoming accustomed to the rolling of the ship's deck. The familiar odor of fish and seawater gave way to the stink of petrol and sewage as Joaquin led the way through narrow canyons of cargo containers. They rounded the corner of a warehouse and came to a concrete bridge connecting the docks to the island on a manmade isthmus. Beyond the bridge, the island rose in rolling hills of emerald green.

He drank in the blessed sight of land. The vast loneliness of being surrounded by nothing but the ocean had brought to life stories of those who went insane at sea. He could understand why.

Joaquin elbowed him and pointed to where a small, bright blue taxi waited on the other side of the bridge. "I called my friend Thomas to take us into the city. POM, as the locals call Port Moresby, is one of the most dangerous cities in the world to visit, but it's safe enough if you have a good driver who knows the city well. We can trust Thomas."

He leaned through the open window to greet the driver before they climbed into the tiny sedan. "Duffy Café," Joaquin told Thomas. He leaned back and turned to Slane. "It's a coffee shop and bakery with a great view of the harbor."

Thomas maneuvered the car along the Napa Napa Road as Slane watched for glimpses of either the city ahead or the harbor to their right. Tall, modern glass buildings rose from the hillside like guardians of the island, protecting it from invaders. Or maybe they were evidence the invaders had already won.

The taxi moved from the commercial docks, past the outskirts of the city where shacks built of discarded wood crowded onto docks, lining the shore to the harbor filled with boats of every size and description.

As they climbed out of the taxi, Slane's friend handed Thomas a few extra coins and asked him to return for them in a couple of hours.

The rich aroma of fresh roasted coffee drew them in. Onboard the ship, the coffee had been passable, but Slane's mouth watered at the thought of the dark, rich brew he had once taken for granted in Prague. Before Bolivia. Before Gerardo. A million lifetimes ago.

Joaquin led the way to the white-tiled counter where fresh baked bread tempted them from behind the glass display. Slane studied the menu hanging behind the counter but didn't recognize any of the food. Hunger softened his resistance to the unknown.

"Have you been here before?" Slane asked his companion.

Joaquin laughed. "Only every time we're in Port Moresby. Best coffee in PNG."

"PNG?"

"It's what we call Papua New Guinea. Port Moresby is the capital city."

"So, what do you recommend?"

"You trust me? I'll order for you."

He'd trusted Joaquin this far, and he didn't have

much choice but to continue despite his wary nature. He pressed his lips into a flat line and lifted his chin in silent assent as Joaquin spoke to the girl behind the counter.

It had been over a month since Slane had seen a woman. The girl's slight figure and dark hair brought Mara's face to mind. But Mara's raven hair framed a much paler face with tear-filled eyes that haunted his dreams. How long had it been? A year and a half. She must think he was dead by now. Maybe she wished he was or, at the least, felt relieved to have him out of her life.

Joaquin elbowed him as the girl repeated the amount he owed for his order. He handed her the two bills the captain had given him, and she passed him several small coins with holes in the center as change. He and Joaquin took their mugs of steaming coffee outside and chose a table with a spectacular view of the harbor.

"How often does the Katie come to Port Moresby?" Slane gazed over the rail at a yacht riding the gentle waves. The beauty of the hills rising in the distance across the bay and the soft, wispy clouds reflected on the sea overcame him like a wave of peace he'd never known. He wrapped his hands, calloused and scarred by his work on the ship, around the mug and sipped the brew. Joaquin wasn't lying. The coffee was good.

Life couldn't get any better than this, could it? Compared to everything he'd known, his hard labor on the ship had been a luxury cruise. Maybe he'd stick with the MSC Katie and try to become an able seaman like Joaquin.

"Our usual route is from here to Busan, South Korea, then back across the Pacific to Manzanillo,

Mexico. We stop in several ports as we move south along the coast of South America, then back across to PNG. That's about two or three months. Sometimes we'll cross the Indian Ocean and make a stop in Mombasa, on the East coast of Africa, or at Karachi or Kandla. It takes about four or five months to make the whole circuit."

"Do you ever get tired of it? I mean, of spending your whole life at sea?"

His friend chuckled. "We get a break occasionally. We sometimes have to make repairs or take care of maintenance on the ship. Then we get shore leave. Some people spend their whole life in one small town. I get to travel around the world several times a year."

The girl who'd taken their order delivered their food, and Slane stared for a moment at the meal his friend had ordered for each of them. A salted bun perched on top of deep-fried chicken covered with a colorful slaw. He lifted the bun and dipped his finger in the sauce to taste it. The aroma of garlic and spices made his mouth water. Beside the "hot chick burger," as the server called it, lay a pile of thick, crispy French fries. Trusting his friend to order for him was definitely the right call.

He took a large bite and closed his eyes for a moment as savory flavor flooded his senses with the tastiest meal he'd had in at least a month. He didn't let the mouthful of food stop him from continuing the conversation. "What do you do on shore leave?" The words were garbled, but Joaquin must have understood.

"Sometimes we sleep on the ship but spend days in the port. Other times I stay with friends I've made in previous visits. But when we're in POM and we have shore leave, that's the best. My uncle has a coffee plantation near the Haedi Training Center and a helicopter he uses to get around the island. He'll come pick me up, and I spend the time helping out on the plantation or at the training center. It gives me the chance to see him and my aunt and a place to stay while I'm on leave."

"Hi-Eddy? Where is that?" Slane wiped his mouth and sipped the strong, rich coffee.

Joaquin smiled as he described his home on the island. "It's north and a little west of here, on the other side of the island, in the Eastern Highlands. The training center houses a satellite campus of the Pacific Institute of Linguistics. Basically, it's a community of people who are working to translate the Bible and other materials into languages the people can understand. Over eight hundred different languages are spoken on this island, so they have a lot of work to do."

More Christians. Like the American girl in Prague and the family he'd met in Bolivia. He'd never known any Christians growing up in his poor neighborhood in Prague, and now they were everywhere he turned. Even Joaquin and the captain had made passing comments about faith and God, leading Slane to suspect they were Christians, too.

"So, is your uncle a Christian?" Slane winced as he heard the bitter hint of accusation in his question. He didn't mean to offend his friend.

Joaquin chewed slowly and waited until he had swallowed to answer. "Yes, he is. And so am I." His gaze latched on to Slane and wouldn't let go for a long, excruciating moment. The riveting, uncomfortable eye contact softened by compassion and kindness caught Slane off guard. His friend looked down at his plate, picked up a fry, and smiled. "What about you?

Who do you believe in?"

Joaquin's choice of words confounded him. Slane let the question swirl around in his head. Not what did he believe, but who did he believe in?

Definitely not his parents. His father abused him and his mother, and she acted as both victim and enabler. He had no friends to believe in. His temper had killed the only relationship he ever had, and he ended up being sold to a drug kingpin as hired muscle. The one friend he'd made in Iquiqui had betrayed him, and he'd just begun to trust Joaquin, but trust was a tenuous thing.

He didn't even believe in himself, although that seemed like the right answer to him. He shrugged and took another bite to avoid answering.

"You seem," Joaquin paused, searching for the words, "I don't know. Like you're seeking something, but you don't know what. Or like you're fighting an enemy you can't see. Maybe you had some bad history with Christians? Do you mind telling me about it?"

Slane looked back toward the water and thought about how far he had come. Halfway around the world and nearly back again. He admitted to himself he'd let bitterness harden his heart. But he knew he didn't have a right to be bitter. He couldn't blame his troubles on anyone but himself. The Christians he'd met had not been perfect, but they wanted to help others. First that girl in Prague, Nicole. She wanted to rescue Mara. From him. And then the family in Santa Cruz had wanted to help Ranza, Hector, and even him. They had no reason to help him. He'd been the enemy, the minion of the man trying to kill them. But they had risked everything to help free him from the cartel. The realization that he alone bore the responsibility for his choices swept over him with a wave of regret.

"It's nothing. Really. My problems are of my own making."

Joaquin nodded, and they ate in relative silence. The muffled sound of chewing their food and washing it down with coffee shrouded their table for several excruciating minutes.

When Slane looked up from his sandwich, Joaquin stared at him again, waiting for him to make eye contact before he spoke.

"Slane, I've spent most of the daylight hours for the past month showing you how to earn your keep and avoid getting yourself killed onboard the ship. I hope I've earned your trust."

Joaquin paused, and Slane pondered how to respond, but his friend waited until he did. He dipped his chin, barely a nod, to acknowledge Joaquin's faithful friendship.

His mentor continued. "I've noticed you seem troubled, and I want to help you get free of whatever seems to be eating you, if I can."

Slane looked away, afraid Joaquin's penetrating gaze would see the demons he'd rather keep locked up. He stuffed a fry, now cold and unappealing, into his mouth and delayed his answer by chewing . Apparently, patience was one of Joaquin's virtues because he waited in silence until Slane knew he'd have to respond. A nod wouldn't satisfy his friend this time.

"Where I come from, my home in Praha, I didn't know any Christians." He began tentatively, but then the words rushed out, and he couldn't hold them back if he wanted to. A dam of emotions burst as he poured out the last eighteen months, which brought him to this moment.

"Because of a Christian, I was beaten and sold like an animal to a drug dealer in South America." His lip curled into a snarl as all the pain he'd endured rushed over him. He paused for a moment to breathe. He hadn't ever said the words out loud. The weight of concealing his story seemed to evaporate with every word. "But I escaped with the help of a family who were also Christians.

"What do I make of that? What am I supposed to think? What kind of God allows the horrible things I've seen … and done? And what kind of God would rescue someone who's done such things?" Heads had turned from nearby tables as his voice rose, and he ducked his chin and lowered his voice. "I don't believe in anyone. Not even myself. The world I've known is a dark place."

Joaquin wiped his mouth and set his napkin aside to lock eyes. Slane read genuine grief in Joaquin's countenance.

Finally, he answered, "I'm so sorry for what you've been through. I don't have any easy answers. But if you trust me, I'll share what I've learned about God. And who knows? Maybe you'll find the answers you're looking for."

Haedi Outpost, Eastern Highlands Province, Papua New Guinea

Amy rose early and sat down at the computer; one foot tucked under her in the chair as she nibbled on a Snax biscuit. At least if she beat the sunrise, she would have a few moments to read updates from her friends on the International Mission Force site before her siblings started clamoring for their turn on the laptop.

She scanned through pictures of faraway places and wondered if her faraway friends also looked at her pictures of Papua New Guinea with longing. Maybe wherever you are always seemed bland compared to some distant, unknown land. "Greener grass" and all that. She didn't want to go anywhere else. She loved this community and the people they served. But that was the problem. She didn't *feel* like she was serving.

Reading updates on the IMF message board from friends in South America and Africa, tears flooded her cheeks at news of the death of one of her online friends. They had never met in person, but it felt like she'd lost a close friend. She imagined what it would be like to face certain death for her faith. Would she be bold and brave, or would she cower and beg for her life? Was her faith strong enough to stand that kind of test? And how would she know what her faith could withstand as long as her life consisted of homework and household chores?

She wanted to give up everything for the call of Christ. That's what her parents had done in coming here, just like missionaries she'd read about her whole life. She lived in this exciting, dangerous, wild place, yet her life seemed inconsequential and ordinary.

It had been a month since her outburst at dinner led to her mom's suggestion she could serve by being a friend to Laila. She'd spent many hours getting to know Laila and helping Laila's mother, Moia, with her two younger children. Amy had learned more Tok Pisin in the past four weeks than in the previous seven years, and she could communicate with Laila as well as with some other girls in the village. A few had come to faith and attended church at the institute, which had a service each week in Tok Pisin. Amy had visited one of the services with them, and she could understand most of the songs, but the message proved more challenging. Her fluency improved daily, but she needed to be doing so much more.

Her hands rested on the keyboard as she considered what more she might do. They were petite and delicate, not suited for hard labor. Whenever they needed a work crew, they were more eager to have her "little" brother Toby's help rather than hers. What could she do of any real value?

She searched the internet for missionary opportunities in Papua New Guinea. Several sites described exciting mission trips into the bush, deep in the rainforest, where few had traveled. Her heart raced as she clicked for more information.

MEN ONLY.

Amy pursed her lips and drew her brows together. Infuriating! She knew all the reasons for limiting female participation on such trips. In addition to primitive and treacherous conditions, the tribes they visited had different values and expectations for women. The rule was intended to protect her. That didn't mean she had to like it.

She scrolled down the page until an article caught her eye. It told the story of a missionary who devoted himself to saving women accused of sorcery, like Moia. Some tribes blamed illness on witchcraft. If a family member became ill or died, they would ask the glasman to identify the witch responsible for their death.

Of course, the glasmen, and their female counterparts, known as glasmeri, were as diverse as the villages they served. Some were herbalists, capable of using generations of knowledge of the flora found on the island to concoct remedies for many illnesses. Others claimed mystical healing powers but were harmless. But some claimed to be able to see spirits, to identify the witch responsible for any death.

Although the glasman might identify a man, most of the time he blamed a woman. Once accused, the tribe would torture her until she confessed to sorcery or named others in a futile effort to save herself. After days of torment, they would burn her alive.

Amy shivered but not from cold. Had Maryann saved Moia from a similar death?

The missionary in the article worked to rescue these women as well as to educate the tribes in order to prevent future retribution, but the cycle of violence continued to grow.

She shuddered at the horror the women must have felt. What would it be like to be falsely accused with no way to prove your innocence? She studied the image of the missionary beside the article as the sun turned the room from gray to golden. What would it be like to save a life?

Wara, Eastern Highlands Province, Papua New Guinea

The glasman lit the bunch of grass clenched in his fist and waved it in wide motions, trailing aromatic smoke in lazy arcs as he chanted the ancient words. He sat cross-legged before the firepit, his face painted and the headdress of brightly colored feathers and delicately carved turtle shells resting on his wiry hair. His gray beard reached to his chest. Below the beard, a hodge-podge of beads, teeth, and stones dangled from a cord strung round his neck. A narrow strip of fabric covered his loins, and his torso, arms, and legs were grayish-white with dried mud from the river bank.

Across the firepit from him stood a stone carving which looked like a miniature statue of himself. It represented one of the myriad spirits he hoped to appease with his offering of a small pig roasting over the fire.

For a full cycle of seasons, his people had been afflicted. Half a dozen of his people had become ill, with dark tumors arising on their skin, and then each had died with great suffering. The tribe looked to him to bring healing. But he had never seen an illness so deadly. And the sprites who used to bring healing were nowhere to be found.

He inhaled the smoke and blew it out through his mouth, closing his eyes as he continued chanting and rocking back and forth. With every breath, his mind wandered to a land where sprites flitted among the sparks of the fire. The sprites used to identify for him the source of the illness, usually a spirit-being disguised as a member of the tribe. He would then point out the person who had been possessed by an evil spirit, and the tribe would execute judgment. The sprites would be satisfied, and the illness would vanish from their tribe.

But this illness was different. In the past, when the sprites identified the culprits and he accused them, the accused would apologize and compensate those they'd wronged by giving them money or pigs in repayment. Or occasionally, they had given him sufficient compensation to make him look the other way. But the rains had been too heavy for their crops.

Only a dozen or so pigs remained in the village, and the burden of his responsibility for the village weighed heavily on him. His sacrifices had not satisfied the spirits, and even worse, the people were beginning to doubt his healing power.

When they were ill, they now went to the missionary woman instead of to him. They trusted in her medicine, and many declared they no longer believed in the sprites or in him.

When their belief in him failed, they would no longer provide for him. He would lose honor in the tribe, as well as provision for his life. More than anything, he feared the tribe turning and executing judgment on him as they had so many times at his direction.

He shuddered at the thought. It was not an easy death.

The missionary woman's face came to mind. She told the people to follow her God and claimed the glasmen and glasmeri did not have magic. She said only her God could heal them. He wished the sprites would point to her as the sanguma; then the villagers could put her to death and be rid of her influence. Perhaps that would satisfy the sprites and secure his position of honor in the tribe again.

CHAPTER THREE

Motukea Island Dockyard, Port Moresby, Papua New Guinea

Slane stretched as he awoke, his arms and legs striking the confines of his berth onboard the Katie. He'd grown accustomed over the past month to sleeping curled into the tight space, just a fraction longer than his height. But upon waking, the hard, metal boundaries rudely reminded him of the limitations of the bunk.

He ran a hand through his tousled hair and pulled on the same worn jeans. The galley buzzed with seamen crowding around the coffee dispenser and jostling for a seat at one of the tables. The captain entered the galley, and the crowd stilled as he strode to a bulletin board and pounded tacks into a notice of shore leave. He turned to face the room as all eyes followed his movements.

"Looks like we're going to be here for a bit, mates. Need some repairs on the diesel engines. Got new head gaskets being flown in from Kuala Lumpur via Singapore. Take at least two weeks for them to arrive, be installed, and then tested. Be sure to let the bosun know how to reach you." Even with his abbreviated sentences, it was the longest speech Slane had heard from the captain.

Joaquin elbowed Slane. "You see? So, now we will have time to visit my uncle. You should come with me. You won't have anything to do here. The city is not a good place to stay by yourself, and you might as well see some of this beautiful island."

Slane shrugged. It sounded like as good a plan as any, and he had no better option. The cramped quarters onboard would get even more cramped after two weeks, and he also couldn't afford a hotel. They gathered their belongings, checked out with the bosun, and disembarked.

Joaquin pulled out his cell phone as they returned to the point where they had met Thomas yesterday. "Uncle Carlos, it's Joaquin."

Slane squinted into the morning sun and tried not to eavesdrop as his friend greeted his uncle. "Yes, I'm in POM. Captain says after the hard seas we weathered; the ship needs several repairs." A brief pause, and then Joaquin responded, "A fortnight. Yes, I can't wait to see you and Aunt Gloria. I also have a friend coming with me." Another pause and Slane stepped away. What if Joaquin's uncle refused? Why should they offer their home to a stranger?

"Thanks. I knew you wouldn't mind. We'll see you at the airport. Vaya con Díos, Tio." He ended the call and slid the phone into his pocket. "We're in luck. He's been in POM on business and was preparing to leave for home when I called. He said they'd be happy to have you join me, and he'll meet us at the airport."

They found Thomas parked near the dock, and he welcomed them back with a smile. Slane slid into the back seat as his friend took the seat beside the driver.

"We need to go to the airport." Joaquin glanced at the time on the dashboard of the taxi. "And we need to get there quickly." He glanced back at Slane. "Thomas will get us to the airport in time," he reassured him though Slane had not asked. As if he had any idea of the distance to the airport, what traffic might be like, or which route to take.

Thomas drove like their lives depended on making it to the airport in record time. The small vehicle darted in and out of traffic, and the driver used the horn with gusto.

They'd almost arrived back in the city when traffic slowed to a crawl, and Slane craned his neck to see what caused the jam. Lights flashed ahead where a police car blocked the lane, and an officer spoke to each driver before waving them on. Thomas inched toward the roadblock. Sweat dotted Slane's forehead, and his mouth dried out. He hadn't violated any law here, but his response stemmed from instinct, not logic. His anxiety had been programmed from an early age in a family culture of petty theft, violence, and dodging law enforcement authorities. The officer approached the open window and spoke to Thomas in words Slane didn't understand. Thomas protested a moment before reluctantly pulling out his wallet and sliding the man thirty kina. The policeman pocketed the bills and waved them through with a smile.

As they pulled away, Slane asked Joaquin, "What was that about?"

Thomas responded, "It is a shake down. Is that what you call it? When a corrupt police officer makes us pay. Sometimes one time a day, sometimes two or three. We must pay or they will put us in jail."

"A bribe?" Slane asked. So PNG was not so far from where he'd been after all.

Thomas and Joaquin laughed at his reaction.

"They refer to taxis as ATMs," Thomas responded. "Because whenever they need cash, they set up a roadblock. They need to pay a bill, they set up a roadblock. You name it, they set up a roadblock." He chuckled without smiling. "Some police officers are honest and good, but some not so much."

Slane recalled the payments he'd delivered for Gerardo to help the police in Santa Cruz look the other way. He shook his head at the corruption which existed everywhere. Even among those who swore to serve and protect.

A few miles later, Thomas zipped past Jacksons Airport and stopped at a hangar beyond the terminals. Joaquin and Slane shouldered their bags and said goodbye to him.

"I'll call to let you know when we need a ride back to the port," Joaquin told his friend as he pulled all the cash from his wallet.

"You can count on me." Thomas smiled broadly as he palmed the bills Joaquin offered, which included the thirty kina the police had demanded as well as the fare for the ride to the airport.

As Thomas pulled away, Slane asked his friend, "Why would you pay so much for a ride to the airport? It took all the money you had left."

"It is worth more to look after my friend, Thomas. He has a family to feed, and he should not have to give up the fare he earned to a corrupt police officer. I can't change the corruption, but I can be sure my friend doesn't suffer because of it. Besides, God has never left me wanting."

Slane recalled Joaquin's similar generosity to him. It was a riddle he had yet to solve. Those who had sworn to protect took advantage of their position, but his friend gave without obligation or expecting anything in return. He gave even when it meant he had nothing left for himself. Yet he didn't seem worried about himself.

Approaching the two ladies at the ticket counter, Joaquin greeted them with a wide smile and a tone suggesting they were old friends.

"Apinun, tupela! Amamas long lukim yutupela!" Slane didn't understand a word his friend said, but apparently the women did.

"Amamas long lukim yu tu!" One of the women hustled around the counter and grasped Joaquin's hand. Their conversation continued, but Slane didn't comprehend a bit of it until Joaquin pointed toward him as he said something about his "gutpela pren." Slane smiled and waved awkwardly, unsure of what Joaquin had said.

Before he had a chance to ask, a man, who must be Uncle Carlos, judging by the resemblance, entered the hangar. His jet-black hair, streaked with silver, and his stocky build painted a picture of Joaquin in twenty years. Joaquin hurried over, and his uncle wrapped him in a bear hug. Slane shifted from one foot to the other as his friend spoke quietly to his uncle, and the older man wiped away tears. It felt like a private moment, and Slane wondered if he should have stayed on the ship after all.

Joaquin turned and introduced them. "Uncle Carlos, this is Slane. He joined us in Peru. He's been learning all about life as an OS."

Slane extended a hand in greeting, and Carlos shook it twice then pulled him into a hug with his free arm. "You are welcome! We are so glad to have you visit us. I spent several years in my youth as a seaman. I recall how precious days ashore are."

"Yes, sir. Thank you." Slane had never used the word "sir" before boarding the MSC Katie, but the month onboard ship in the company of Joaquin had left its mark.

"Go ahead and stow your bags. We'll depart shortly."

Joaquin led Slane out of the hangar past a row of

various aircraft. Slane had never flown in his life and didn't know what to expect, but when his friend stopped at a helicopter not much larger than a minivan, Slane stopped in his tracks.

"We're flying in that?" He stood ten feet from the chopper with his feet planted wide.

Joaquin opened the small door on the side and secured his bag behind the seats. "Yes, I've flown with my uncle many times. He is a very good pilot."

Slane didn't move. "I'm not worried about the pilot; I'm worried about the plane."

Uncle Carlos slipped up behind him. "It's not a plane. It's a helicopter. You do not need to worry about her. She may be nearing retirement, but she still has a few good years left, eh, Joaquin?"

Slane's face warmed at being overheard.

Joaquin tugged at his arm again, and Slane folded his tall frame into the small seat behind the pilot while his friend took the seat beside his uncle. The pilot paced around the aircraft, inspecting every inch as he called out several things which made no sense to Slane, followed by the word "check."

"He is completing his pre-flight inspection," Joaquin explained. "You see? Perfectly safe. Fasten your seatbelt." His friend gestured to the lap belt, and Slane eagerly complied. Joaquin handed him a headset as well. "This will let us communicate once he starts the engine, and it will protect your ears from the noise."

Carlos climbed in and finished checking various gauges before reviewing pre-flight safety instructions with his passengers. When he mentioned the seat could be used as a flotation device, Slane's heart raced and sweat beaded on his brow.

Finally, Carlos started the engine as Joaquin and

Slane settled the headsets over their ears. Even with the protection, the muffled thwop-thwop of the blades and the roar of the engine drowned out any other noise.

When the chopper rose from the asphalt, Slane considered praying for the first time in his life. The nose of the tiny chopper dipped as it lifted off, and Slane's body angled forward, then pressed back against the seat as the chopper gained speed. His fingers curled around his knees. When they cleared the height of the airport, his heart dropped into his shoes and remained there for most of the flight.

The roar of the rotor spinning overhead allowed little opportunity for conversation without shouting even through the headset, so he fixed his eyes on the window. The city below shrank from view and gave way first to lowlands and then to steep, green mountains, lush in vegetation and dotted with thatched-roof huts clustered in tiny villages. A steep gorge provided views of a waterfall plunging three hundred feet into a milky green pool below.

Joaquin pointed as if Slane could possibly miss the sight and shouted, "Rouna Falls. Beautiful, yes?"

Slane nodded. He'd never seen such rich, emerald green as the jungles below. The wooded parks of Prague boasted darker shades of evergreens, and the portions of Bolivia he had encountered featured burnt orange deserts more than forests. The Salar de Uyuni had offered a flat, unbroken reflection of the heavens as far as the eye could see, and the mountains he'd climbed to pass from Bolivia into Chile were beautiful. But this view took his breath away. Narrow ribbons of road marked the rugged terrain as they flew across the island to the highlands.

Carlos's voice in his headset announced their

arrival in Haedi. Slane frowned and craned his neck, trying to make out a city, or at least an airport, but only a dark orange strip of dirt stood out amongst the green. Carlos ignored the dirt runway and continued until they hovered over a small opening in the tree canopy. On one side of the clearing, a state-of-the-art log cabin with a green tin roof nestled among the dark foliage. While the colors and materials blended with the natural environment, the modern style and satellite dish seemed at odds with the remote location. The ground bore a rough circle of dirt in the midst of the opening in the trees. That small circle appeared to be Carlos's target.

Slane renewed his grip on his knees and closed his eyes as the chopper dropped until he felt a mild jolt. For an instant he thought they'd crashed, his life screeching to a halt here, on an island in the Pacific far from home. Regret washed over him like a tidal wave. So many moments he wished he could do over. But when he opened his eyes, they'd safely landed on the ground and Joaquin grinned back at him.

A plump, tanned woman in a flowing dress of bright, geometric patterns came out of the cabin to greet them. Joaquin wrapped his arms around her thick waist and lifted her easily off the ground for a moment before turning to Slane. "Aunt Gloria, this is our newest OS, Slane."

Slane reached out a hand, but the smiling woman grabbed his arm and pulled him into a bone-crushing hug. "Welcome to Kopi!"

Slane and Joaquin grabbed the small bags they'd brought and followed her into the house as Carlos announced his plans to check on the coffee production.

Gloria led them through a large gathering room

featuring a stone fireplace on one wall. The exposed logs of the cabin glowed with a bright, clean polish, and the furniture spoke of warm family times by the fire. The wide wooden staircase led to a loft overlooking the main room, and two bedrooms branched off from the loft and shared a bathroom. She showed them each to a room and pointed out the fresh towels in the bathroom.

"I'll let the two of you have thirty minutes or so to rest from the trip while your uncle finishes his rounds and then dinner should be ready. Welcome, Slane." She smiled and headed down the stairs.

Slane stood alone in the room, turning slowly to take in everything. The room dwarfed his family's apartment in Prague and smelled of coffee beans and vanilla instead of alcohol and sweat. The polished wood of the furniture matched the walls, and a brightly colored woven rug warmed the floor.

A ring hung from the ceiling, draped with mosquito netting which encompassed the bed. And what a bed! It looked like a heavenly cloud compared to the bunk he'd had onboard, and he couldn't resist sitting on the edge and then laying back in the luxurious softness.

He didn't recall ever being surrounded by such abundance. He'd had glimpses of it once when he walked Mara home, and in the hotel where he'd worked in Chile, but he'd never experienced it himself. He must be dreaming. Surely he'd wake up and find himself lying in a pile of rags, waiting for more abuse from Gerardo, or his kidnappers, or even his own father.

He shut his eyes tight, hoping to barricade his imagination against the onslaught of memories, but still the images replayed. Snapping his eyes open again and drinking in the comfort of the room brought a moment of relief. At least he was here, now.

Wara, Eastern Highlands, Papua New Guinea

Toby pulled the door to Miss Maryann's tiny home closed behind him and his brother, and they started down the path toward Haedi. She had plenty of stories to tell, and she'd looked a little disappointed when he cut her off with an excuse about needing to get home. He'd planned for this day, going back and forth between how to find time for exploration and weighing the potential consequences if anyone caught him. Or worse yet, if his curiosity proved to be as dangerous as his mother had warned him so many times.

His fingers brushed against the bone he kept in his pocket. It had become a source of fascination, almost to the point of obsession. Still, he'd managed to keep it hidden, even from Brandon. It wouldn't do for his brother to discover what he had planned.

He waited until they had walked about thirty minutes from the village before launching his plan.

"Oh man! I forgot my watch. I took it off when I helped Miss Maryann in her garden. I've got to go back and get it."

"We don't have time to go back. Wait and get it next time." Just as Toby expected, Brandon refused to go back for it.

"No, it will be a whole week! Just wait here. I'll run; it won't take long."

His brother drew a long sigh. Toby had known what his response would be. In fact, he had counted on it.

"You go back and get it. I'll walk slow. You can catch up with me."

Perfect! Toby almost shouted it but forced himself to shrug and sigh, feigning reluctance as he turned back the way they'd come and set out at a jog. Over a small rise in the path, out of sight of his brother, he slowed to a walk and searched for the spot where he had found the bone.

He pulled his watch from his pocket and strapped it on his wrist. A slight twinge of guilt over his lie plagued him, but he justified it easily. Brandon had lied plenty of times.

The wooded area lay near where he'd left Brandon. If any serious danger arose and he screamed loud enough, his brother would hear him. At least, if his brother really kept a slow pace. And if Toby didn't get lost in the woods.

He found the spot along the path where he'd noticed a narrow trail winding among the trees and followed it to discover the bone. Was it the secrecy of his plan that made the hair on his neck rise, or was he being watched? He took a few dozen steps off the path into the woods and began scanning the undergrowth for the log which marked the place he'd found the bone.

A twig snapped nearby, and his heart raced.

"Hello?" He called. Instantly annoyed by the squeaky, little-boy sound of his voice, he lowered his tone, "Brandon, is that you?"

A rustling in the brush sent him scurrying behind a tree where he cowered for several minutes, peering through the dense green foliage in search of the source of the noise.

A cassowary stepped out onto the path. It cocked

its turquoise head to one side and fixed its amber eyes upon him as if trying to figure him out. The dark gray casque rose three inches tall like a prehistoric shield between those golden orbs. The flightless bird stood nearly as tall as Toby. The muscular legs narrowed to skinny, chicken-like feet with a five-inch-long claw at the end of one toe. It reminded Toby of an old movie about dinosaurs being resurrected in modern times. The wispy black feathers wavered in the slight breeze — the only motion for several long moments as Toby dared not breathe.

The bird spread its wings and raised its head, leading with its breast. It turned at an angle, about forty-five degrees to Toby, and took a couple steps closer. Toby had seen the maneuver before on a chess board. The bird moved toward his flank in order to attack from the side. It let out a noise, a warning sound which reminded Toby of someone huffing in indignation. The deep red wattle swayed with each movement.

Stories flashed through his mind of humans attacked, the long, lethal claw ripping into their skin. What advice had the article given for surviving a confrontation? He drew a blank. Should he shout and try to scare it off? Climb a tree to escape it? Turn and run away? The image of the raptor-like bird leaping on his back rendered his feet immovable.

An eerie howling in the distance sent a flock of lorikeets rising from the trees in a rush of brilliant green, flapping wings and screeching like nails on a chalkboard. They swept through an opening in the canopy of trees, and when Toby's gaze returned to the woods, the cassowary had evaporated.

Had he imagined it? He shook his head as if trying to rouse himself from a dream. He'd studied about cassowaries. They didn't live near people. What were the odds he would see one this close to the village? His imagination must be getting the best of him.

The howl continued and trailed off into a piercing high note. That was real enough. It might have been a wild dog, but the keening cry sounded almost human. Toby hurried back to the trail he'd taken into the woods, glancing over his shoulder and praying whatever made that ungodly noise wasn't following him.

The howling continued but faded as he left it behind. He'd been searching for an hour when he came to the spot where he had found the tiny bone. Brandon might be wondering why he hadn't caught up with him by now. Probably not.

He looked around, wondering if someone might have pursued him or he might encounter a stranger on this remote trail. Brandon might have doubled back to find him. Thick growth of broadleaf evergreens surrounded him. He scuffed his tennis shoes through the leaves and underbrush, looking for any evidence of where the bone came from but also terrified of what he might find.

Step by step, he moved deeper into the rainforest. The woods were still and silent. The creatures held their breath. A few more feet and he'd turn back. This was nuts. But his heart raced, and adrenalin rushed through him as it had before.

Then his foot struck something hard among the undergrowth. His hand trembled as he reached down to pull back the leafy branches covering the forest floor. The sight of a reddish-brown skull sent him stumbling backward until he landed hard on his backside. He leapt to his feet and desperately tried to re-trace his path through the brush to the trail. A million wild noises broke the silence, which had engulfed him a moment before. Birds called through the trees. Insects chirped and whirred around him. The howling he'd thought he had escaped echoed in the distance.

Where was the trail? His breath came in ragged gasps as he tried to get his bearings. The patches of wooded areas in the highlands weren't large. He should be able to find his way out and to the edge of the gorge. Had he gotten turned around? Was he even headed toward the path or deeper into the woods?

A sob welled up and stuck in his throat. He clung to the lichen-covered bark of a tree which stretched a hundred feet into the sky. The trees around him closed in like sentries guarding age-old secrets. Guarding the grave of the victim he'd found. The thick foliage of impenetrable shades of green and brown stretched in every direction.

Then he glimpsed a lighter shade—a shaft of sunlight breaking through the canopy. His heart leapt. It had to be the trail. He raced through the trees toward the light, his adventure forgotten and home his only quest.

When he emerged from the gloom, joy overwhelmed him. Relief as powerful and tangible as a wave breaking over him fueled his flight. He raced down the path until he felt his heart would explode. He paused for a moment. Air burned as he sucked it into his lungs, his hands planted on his knees. After what seemed a lifetime, his heart rate returned to a manageable pace, and he resumed his trek down the side of the mountain.

The bridge across the gorge loomed ahead, and his anxiety about what he'd just experienced empowered him to race across it. He didn't take the time to think about it but hurried across with his hands skimming along the rope.

He caught up to Brandon as they came in sight of the gate, and the sky faded from blue to purple.

"What took you so long, little dude? And how'd you get leaves stuck in your hair?" The mocking tone belied any concern about his safety. Brandon rose lightning-fast onto his toes and wrapped his arm around Toby's neck, doubling him over, and rubbing his knuckles on Toby's head as he had when Toby was little.

But Toby wasn't a kid anymore.

He elbowed Brandon in the gut and jerked out of the embrace, a fierce scowl answering his brother's questions. Brandon shrugged, and the two hurried on in silence through the gate.

Amy glanced up from taking in laundry off the line in the yard to see Toby and Brandon hustling through the gate and down the lane toward the house.

"What's your hurry?" She yelled as they passed by.

Brandon ignored her and went inside, but Toby paused. His face flushed, a twig poked out of his unruly black curls, and he panted for breath. He looked like he might cry. Or maybe have a heart attack. He crossed the space and stood beside her, bent over as he waited a minute to catch his breath.

"You okay?" She reached out and plucked the leaf from his hair and tossed it aside.

He cast his eyes from side to side and said, "You promise not to say anything to mom and dad?"

"Of course not." She frowned. His expression said he wanted to tell her anyway but mentally weighed the consequences.

"Just go ahead and spill the beans. You know you can't keep a secret, Toby."

He folded his arms across his chest and pressed his lips together. She'd clearly offended him. "Hmph. Oh, yeah? Watch me." With stubborn defiance, he turned his back on her and stomped toward the house. He even ignored Bublé.

Amy shrugged. Probably sweet on some girl in his class or found something gross in the woods. Who cares about a fourteen-year-old boy's secrets?

She finished her chore and carried the laundry inside to fold it. So much for her grand service for the kingdom of God.

As she sat on the sofa pulling clothes from the woven grass basket, her mother returned from the market with a bilum bag filled with fruit. As she unloaded it, she held up three matching, brightly flowered meri blauses and announced, "Look what I found for us to wear to the singsing tomorrow?"

Amy laughed. "We'll look like a walking garden!"

"Actually, we'll blend in a little better than we did last year." Her mother laughed. Amy agreed. Last year, they had looked more like the tourists who came to gawk and take pictures of the various tribes showing off their regalia than like those who made PNG their home.

Fun-filled memories of the annual cultural festival in Goroka brought a smile to her face. For a change in scenery and the excitement of the festival, she'd wear whatever her mom wanted. The singsing provided a chance to see and celebrate the immense variety of cultures represented on one island. Amy loved the bustling kaleidoscope of colors and costumes and languages. What excitement would this year's festival hold?

CHAPTER FOUR

Kopi Plantation

Slane awoke to the sound of Joaquin banging on the door, calling his name, and bright morning sunlight filtering through the window. He stretched like a lazy cat and relished the sensation of freedom and space to fully extend his fingers and toes. His stomach rumbled, a reminder that he'd never gone down to the dinner Gloria promised the night before. At some point, he had at least drawn his feet up onto the bed, but he hadn't even taken off his shoes.

He jumped up and ran his hands through the shaggy hair which hung to his shoulders. Opening the door, he apologized for missing dinner.

"I know how it is when you see a real bed for the first time in a month. My aunt and uncle do, too. You were so sound asleep, I let you rest, amigo."

"Thanks. But my stomach is not nearly as forgiving." He rubbed his flat stomach, and it let out a growl in agreement.

Joaquin laughed. "Let's see what we can do."

The two hustled down the stairs and into the kitchen where Gloria stood over a small stove flipping pancakes that looked a little off-color, but at this point Slane would eat anything.

"Good morning. I would say I hope you slept well, but I suppose good sleep is guaranteed after a month at sea." She set a plate filled with the light brown pancakes in front of him. "They're sago pancakes. You'll find we eat a lot of sago and kaukau here. I hope you like them."

Slane scooped up a helping of mango and put it on top of the pancakes before taking a large bite. Different, but his appetite heightened their flavor. He had finished half the plate by the time the others sat down with their plates. When Carlos bowed his head and reached for his wife's hand to pray over the meal, Slane paused chewing and looked down at his plate. When they finished, he apologized.

"Sorry. Didn't mean to be rude."

"Not at all. You were hungry. It's a compliment to see you enjoying the meal." Gloria patted his hand across the table.

Carlos changed the subject. "I thought maybe we would drive over to Goroka for the singsing tomorrow, but today, I'll show you where the coffee you're drinking comes from."

Joaquin pumped his fist as he swallowed a bite of pancake. "That sounds great! It's been so long since I've been to the festival. My trips never seem to be timed quite right for it. " He punched Slane's arm. "You are in for quite an experience."

"What is a singsing?" Slane sipped the fresh coffee and pictured them all dressing in choir robes and singing church songs. Had coming with Joaquin to visit his Christian aunt and uncle been a mistake?

"Every year at this time, tribes come from many miles away for a cultural festival. They dress in their traditional regalia and perform dances passed down in their clans for thousands of years. It is a chance to see something few people ever experience for themselves." Carlos stabbed another bite of mango and waved his fork at Joaquin and Slane. "You two are very lucky."

With breakfast finished, Slane enjoyed a long, hot shower — another precious luxury. Afterward, Carlos led them from the house to where the pulping machine processed the coffee cherries his workers had picked the day before. Joaquin pointed to a tank filled with berries soaking in water and explained, "After they pulp the coffee cherries, they are moved to the fermentation tank to soak for a day or two before being spread to dry. While they are drying, they must be turned regularly to ensure they dry evenly. Before we transport them to the port, they will have the parchment hull removed and be hand-checked for quality and size. Finally, they are stored in bags to be shipped to the port."

Despite all the coffee Slane had consumed, he'd never considered how it arrived at the little *potraviny* on the corner of his street in Praha. His lack of appreciation for all the labor required to provide every cup of coffee brought an unfamiliar twinge of guilt. What was this foreign sense of empathy for the efforts and feelings of strangers? It was their job.

Carlos greeted the team leader for the workers who were processing the bright red coffee cherries through the pulping machine. A woman clad in a bright shirt and printed floral wrap skirt dumped scoops of the previous day's crop into the hopper, and the pulped cherries dropped from the bottom into a large basket. As the last of the cherries dropped from the machine, the woman cleaned the machine in preparation for today's harvest. Carlos spoke to the foreman and inspected the results of their labor. Joaquin led Slane to where five more women in bright dresses sat, inspecting and sorting the coffee beans spread all around them on the woven mat.

"Any bean damaged in processing, spoiled, or eaten by insects has to be rejected." Carlos explained when he joined them. "We have very strict quality standards. If the number of defects in our supply increases, we'd lose the contracts we have and go out of business. It's taken years to establish a reputation for providing the best, but it only takes one bad lot for your reputation to be ruined."

Slane wondered if Carlos referred to the coffee or something more. In a little over a day, Joaquin's uncle had shown Slane more kindness than his father ever mustered and had also shared more wisdom. How might his life have turned out if he'd had a father like Carlos?

Carlos pulled a couple of buckets from the storage building and showed Slane and Joaquin where to begin. They joined the workers under the areca trees, and Joaquin showed him the difference between the yellow coffee cherries and the deep red, almost purple ones that were ripe.

Slane glanced at the other workers, mostly women, some with babies hanging on their backs in one of those woven bags. They greeted him with a smile but never paused in the rhythm of picking handfuls of the ripe cherries and dropping them in their bucket.

Slane and Joaquin picked for several hours and then took a break and returned to the house, where Gloria had prepared lunch for them. They returned to fill several more buckets in the afternoon. By the time the sun rested on the mountains in the west, Slane's hands were raw and his back ached from stooping to reach cherries in the lower branches. They waited in line with the women to turn in their buckets and have them weighed. He had picked perhaps a hundred pounds of the cherries, about half what the experienced women had harvested.

As they ambled back to the house, he stretched his aching back and asked Joaquin, "Do you always work so much during your time off?"

Joaquin shuffled a few more steps before he answered. "When I was nine, my parents both died. We were very poor, and it took time before word reached my uncle about what had happened. I had nowhere to live, so I lived on the streets. When my uncle learned I had been orphaned, he traveled all the way to South America. He searched until he found me. He brought me here to live, and it was paradise after the places I had lived." He swung his arms wide as he gestured to the plantation. "He provided everything for me from then on. And even now, if I stayed, he would give me anything I asked." He grinned at Slane.

"Carlos never asks me to work when I'm here. I volunteer because I love them, and it makes me happy to help them. I could never repay them for all they've given me. They don't need our help. They have all the workers they need and can hire more workers if they need more, because the people in the valley know my uncle is a generous man who treats his employees well."

Slane nodded but remained silent. Would he ever understand this new friend of his? The idea of working this hard when it wasn't required or even asked seemed as foreign to him as everything he had seen on this island.

Haedi Outpost, Eastern Highlands Province, Papua New Guinea

"Time to get up!" His mother's voice pulled Toby from a deep sleep where he had tracked the glasman through the woods, trying to catch him in his magic. He shook off the lingering sensation that the dream had been real.

"We need to head out soon if we are going to make it to Goroka for the singsing." She poked her head in the door and repeated. "Time to get up, Toby."

He rolled out of bed and threw on some clothes. His newfound interest in tribal culture made today's event especially exciting. Representatives from tribes across the highlands and even as far as the coast would show off traditional song and dance. They would be dressed as they had for centuries, in their most impressive paint, feathers, and garb. He would get to see them performing rituals they had practiced pretty much forever. Maybe he'd even see the glasman from Wara.

They piled into the Mule and waited with several other families near the gate. Mr. Dan joined them with one of the few vehicles in the community, an ancient Volkswagen camper painted with bright-colored artwork. Along with a few other trucks and vans, they would caravan to bring people from the institute to Goroka for the singsing and then back late that night. They packed each vehicle full and headed out the gate over roads riddled with potholes, but Toby welcomed the luxury of riding rather than walking.

The drive took an hour, and crowds had packed

the town by the time they arrived. Dozens of tribes had already assembled. They sat in clusters on the dusty field in the center of the village, each tribe member creating a special headdress for the occasion. The festival would last four days, with many tribes traveling days by foot to participate. Ninety groups with nearly a thousand participants crowded the field.

Toby's family parked with others from Haedi near the field, and Toby followed his parents and siblings into the arena. They searched out a spot with a good view of the field and settled onto their blanket on the grass to eat the traditional lunch included with their tickets.

Toby pulled out his journal as the first group took the field, sporting beards painted white and headdresses in brilliant red, turquoise, and white feathers. Around their bare chests hung a white crescent-shaped kina shell, framed in red and edged with green leaves. Woven bands around their biceps held more leaves, and their exposed skin glistened in the mid-day sun. Toby's glasses slid down his nose as he sketched the figures.

When the drums started, Toby's heart pounded in time with them. The excitement and tension of the elaborate dance conveyed both a ritual and a demonstration of their power to other tribes.

He set aside his journal and picked at the plate of mumu his mother handed him. He preferred the steamed pork and rice to the kaukau, and pushed the greens off to the side of his plate, wrinkling his nose. The next group taking their places drew his attention to the field. This was his favorite! The mud men.

As their name implied, the mud men had coated their bodies in a light gray mud, and each wore a large mask covering their entire head. Sharpened bamboo shoots were tied to each finger. As they stepped forward, lifting their knees high, they clicked the bamboo together in an unsettling rhythm. Instead of the frenetic dance he'd just seen, they intimidated their opponents with their slow, deliberate march. Toby shivered. It worked.

Amy sat cross-legged on the blanket, eating her lunch with her fingers and trying to avoid looking at the Papuan women whose costumes included only jewelry and paint from the waist up. It seemed awkward to her, but they appeared to be completely at ease. In contrast, the women in Haedi, the village near their community, wore meri blauses, like the ones her mom bought, and long skirts. She'd seen mothers sitting outside their home nursing their baby, but never walking about topless. These women wore shells strung in thick drapes around their neck or layers of brightly colored paint to conceal their flesh. But how on earth did they do their dances, jumping up and down as they did?

Thinking of the women and babies in the village sparked an idea. Perhaps she could serve by helping with their babies. Many of them worked at the coffee plantation and took their babies along in bilum bags slung on their back, but maybe Amy could help tend the older babies.

Her little sister Ruth had been born a year after they moved to Haedi, when Amy was ten. She had loved playing with her, feeding her a bottle, and taking care of her while her mom helped at the clinic. She didn't have many opportunities to babysit at the institute, not for a lack of children, but rather a lack of opportunities for the parents to go out without them.

She looked up from her plate and her musings to see the next group taking the field. The men wore blue skirts, or at least the front looked like a skirt, but as they passed by, the sides gaped and revealed their leg, from thigh to ankle, painted white. A large red plate with a golden crescent representing the kina shell covered their bare chests. Red and yellow paint coated their faces so thickly she couldn't distinguish any features, and each of their unique headdresses featured long black feathers standing at least eighteen inches above their head. They moved in unison, stomping the ground as they came onto the field and whistling through some type of reed in their mouths.

She'd been to the festival each year since they'd arrived, and the detail and pageantry still overwhelmed her. Encountering one of those warriors in a battle, with their stone axes and bow and arrows, would be terrifying.

But if she helped the mothers in Haedi, perhaps she wouldn't feel so much like a spectator. She'd spent her whole life watching, rather than serving.

"Amy!" A familiar voice called her name, and she craned her neck to find the source. It couldn't be! It had been at least six months since Joaquin's last visit, and she was jealous of his freedom, but she'd recognize his voice anywhere.

Still not seeing him, she jumped to her feet and shielded her eyes against the mid-day sun as she searched the crowd for her pseudo-big brother.

Brandon might be her older brother, but Joaquin had taken the role of her protector, champion, and hero shortly after they had moved to PNG. They'd been at Haedi for a few months when she got a letter from a friend in the states which brought on a powerful bout of homesickness. The combination of reading about her friends back home having fun together and feeling out of place in this strange new home had crushed her with a one-two punch of grief. She'd ran out of the school and hid behind a bush to pour out her tears.

Joaquin had passed by just then and heard her. Four years older than her, he'd been her age when he lost his parents. He'd moved in with his uncle halfway around the world, so he understood how it felt to lose everything familiar. He also had the uncanny ability to turn her tears into laughter. His antics had driven away her homesickness. From that day on, it seemed like he had made it his personal mission to make her smile.

Whether pulling a prank on himself, or on someone else, he'd stop at nothing to provoke a chuckle. She scanned the crowd again. He had to be here somewhere. Unfortunately, a tourist who had to be at least six feet tall blocked her view and squelched any hope of finding him.

Just when she thought she would have to give up or ask the towering beanpole to please sit down or step aside, Joaquin popped out from behind him with a loud shout and a mask over his face. Amy screamed, then squealed in delight and dissolved into giggles.

Joaquin handed the mask back to its owner with a quick thank you and swung her into a bear hug. He spun her around until her knees buckled as he set her on her feet. She leaned on his arm to steady herself.

"I can't believe you're here! How long will you be home? Has it been wonderful being at sea? Where have you gone this time?"

He laughed and held up both hands as if protecting himself from her rapid-fire interrogation.

"Hang on a minute. I'll fill you in, but I want to introduce our latest OS, and my friend, Slane." He turned and indicated the tourist she had just contemplated taking out at the knees.

Her neck arched as her eyes trailed from his chest up to his face, where a shaggy lock of brown hair covered half his face. The other half revealed an expression of eagerness mixed with trepidation. Was this giant afraid of the tribe performing a war ritual for the festival? Or of her?

He shook her hand, and she caught a change in expression, a glint in his eye. As if the touch had shocked him with static electricity. She pulled her hand back and tried to cover her unease. "It's nice to meet you, Slane." But as the name rolled off her lips, she had the sudden, distinct impression she should recognize it.

She stared at his face, searching for whether she'd met him before. "Where are you from? I mean, originally. Your name seems unusual, or at least unusual for PNG." She shrugged.

"I caught the MSC Katie in Peru. But my home is Praha."

"You've come a long way."

A loud roar interrupted their conversation as one of the crowd favorites entered the field. The Huli tribe, sporting elaborate wigs and bright yellow faces painted with ambua, a yellow clay considered sacred by the tribe, entered the field.

"Come sit with us!" Amy grabbed Joaquin's arm and pulled him over to join her family. His friend trailed behind with eyes wide as saucers at the sights around him. Drums cut short their greetings and introductions as the Huli tribe began to dance to the steady, unified beating of the drums each of them carried.

Amy had grown accustomed to the powerful impact of the performances, but she smiled as she caught the expression of awe on Slane's face at witnessing it for the first time. He glanced her way, and she jerked her gaze back to the field as her face flushed at being caught staring.

Why did his name seem so unusual, but so familiar?

Slane folded his legs and sat on the ground behind his friend and the blonde who had taken his breath away. His gaze cut from her to the field. He stared as the men, covered in red paint, with palm fronds sticking out of the back of their waistband like giant rooster tails, hopped to the beat of the drum. Their simple dance, combined with the elaborate costume and somber expressions covered in yellow and red paint, would intimidate any foe.

Fear was the point, right? No matter where he went, the common goal of every culture seemed to be domination, intimidation, and control. It had been his father's sole purpose in life. Mara's father had been the same. The thugs who'd kidnapped him, Gerardo, even these tribes who were relatively untainted by Western culture, they all had this innate quest for dominance in common.

He glanced at his friend, Joaquin. Except him. Joaquin hadn't asked for anything. As Slane's superior onboard the ship, Joaquin had the authority to give orders which Slane must follow, but Joaquin never misused his authority. The faces of the family who had helped him escape Gerardo also came to mind.

Peter and Kasey. They had demanded nothing, and they had every reason to distrust him and leave him in the salt flat for dead. Without a doubt, Joaquin and Peter and Kasey stood apart from the world in which he'd grown up. The only world he'd ever known.

The stunning girl Joaquin had just introduced him to leaned toward him and pointed at the dancers. "Their dance and costumes mimic the bird of paradise. See how the palm branches and the leaves in their armbands kind of look like feathers and wings?" She didn't touch him, but her face drew so near it felt like an electric current ran through the tiny space separating them.

The clean, natural scent of her hair surrounded him. She was beautiful, but not in a polished, fake sort of way. Her short blonde hair twisted in little strands, which framed her face perfectly. Her skin needed no makeup, and a few freckles dotted her nose. Crystal blue eyes lined by thick, dark lashes created the look plenty of girls paid cosmetic companies to create.

She raised her eyebrows at him. "What?"

He'd been staring, lost in the ocean of her eyes.

"Oh, nothing. I'm sorry." He looked back at the field, suddenly conscious that other than the girl at the coffee shop yesterday and Joaquin's aunt, he hadn't seen a female in a month.

His friend's elbow connected with a rib. Joaquin whispered, "Be careful. Those are some dangerous waters you're diving into, my friend."

Slane grinned. He had been drawn toward danger his entire life.

What were they whispering about? Amy

pretended to shift her position to get more comfortable, but she concentrated on trying to hear Joaquin's comment to his friend over the pounding of the drums.

No use.

The way Slane stared at her disrupted her usually quiet demeanor. The intensity of his dark gaze felt like standing on the precipice of a deep well, about to fall into oblivion.

She tried to ignore him, to focus instead on the dancers, her family, the beautiful sunny day. But her attention drifted time after time back to this enigma. As the Huli tribe finished and they waited for the next group to perform, she asked Joaquin, "How long will you be home?"

"We have a fortnight of shore leave this time. I can tell you, it is good to be home, even if only a couple of weeks."

Slane winced and cast his eyes toward the mountain, reacting to the comment like a blow, his jaw set like a little boy trying to be tough. She eased away from the topic of home.

"Do you two have any big plans while you're here?"

"You're looking at it." Joaquin chuckled. "This. And helping on the plantation. And lots of sleep, right, Slane?"

His friend laughed and seemed to turn a little pink under his suntanned skin.

Amy's mom leaned over and put a hand on Slane's shoulder. "We'll have to have the two of you, and Carlos and Gloria, over for dinner one night this week." Amy smiled at her mom's hospitality. Of course, they'd known Joaquin for years, and her mother would invite a stranger in, regardless.

Surprise registered on Slane's face, as if an invitation into someone's home whom he'd just met amazed him.

"Thank you." The drums of the next tribe drowned out his reply. They marched in, knees high, and steps as synchronized as a drill team. This tribe, like the Huli, each carried a long, narrow drum across their torso, which they beat in time. They wore garments resembling burlap sacks woven from tree bark similar to bilum bags and bound at the waist with leaves. Amy offered another explanation to the newcomer. "The skirt they wear is called a yambal, and they are at least seven layers thick. That's what makes them follow their movements, see?" She pointed to the dancers and the fluid movements of their garments. "The piece that looks almost like a necktie is called a boingke. It's made of horizontal pieces of bamboo strung together, and it keeps a tally of all the pigs owed to you by other members of the tribe."

Slane listened intently, so she continued. "Their headdresses are made of real human hair. See how they look like giant black mushrooms? And the part edged in white? That is a tail feather from a ribbon-tailed astrapia."

He leaned forward, and his calloused hand brushed her arm as he pointed beyond the performers to where the next group prepared to enter the field. "What about that group?"

The tribe wore black paint over their whole body, with white paint illustrating an accurate and detailed skeleton on their face and body.

"That is the Chimbu tribe. They developed their paint to scare off rival tribes who tried to attack them. Now it's viewed as a way of celebrating their culture."

Amy relaxed as the volume of the performances limited the opportunity for small talk. Something about Joaquin's companion both intrigued and discomforted her and, try as she might, she couldn't pinpoint it. His presence, close behind her because of the crowd, made her stomach tense as if she were alone with the stranger. The intensity in his gaze, the contrast of her size relative to his, and a feeling of his strength being barely contained unnerved her.

Ruth crawled over and sat in Amy's lap backwards, resting her chin on her older sister's shoulder as she stared at the newcomer. Out of the corner of her eye, Amy glimpsed her sister reaching for the edge of his sleeve. Before she could stop her, Ruth had lifted it a few inches, revealing a tattoo of a snake wrapped around his biceps and poised to strike. Amy recoiled at the image, but Ruth traced it with her finger.

"Why did you paint a snake on your arm?" The six-year-old had seen plenty of tattoos among the tribes here at the festival and those who lived in Haedi, but nothing like this.

Slane pulled the sleeve back down, looking around as if afraid others would see. "It's nothing." He frowned, but his voice held more sorrow than anger. "And I didn't paint it. Someone else 'painted' it on me." He crossed his arms and covered the tattoo with his hand.

"I'm sorry. They shouldn't have done that if you didn't want them to." Her little sister viewed everything in such simple terms. Undeterred by Slane's reaction, she continued. "A boy in my class tried to draw on my arm with a marker, and I told the teacher. She made him 'pologize.'"

A smile tugged at the corners of Slane's mouth.

Nobody could stay somber under Ruth's relentless joy. Oblivious to his discomfort, the little girl pulled the sleeve up again and traced the snake with her finger, then kissed her finger and touched the head of the snake. "I don't like snakes, but I like you. You seem nice." With that pronouncement, she rose from Amy's lap and squirmed between her sister and Joaquin to plop down on the knees of this stranger.

Amy chuckled at the stunned look on his face. Her tension eased a tiny bit. How bad could he be if Ruth approved?

Toby rolled his eyes at the conversation between his sister and this new guy, Joaquin's friend. Now Ruth had climbed over Amy to talk to him. Leave it to Ruth. She'd talk to anyone.

Girls! Whether six or sixteen, he thought, all they seemed interested in were boys.

Not that he wasn't interested in the girls in his class at school, but plenty of other things captured his attention. He sat with his journal open on his knees, jotting notes about each of the tribes. He'd read an article online about their cultures and customs, but it didn't capture the impact of seeing them in person. In the margins, he sketched images of their costumes. Weird and different, some of them terrifying, but all fascinating, and he wanted to learn more. Perhaps understanding the tribes would shed light on the bone he found in the woods.

He added a note beside the Huli tribe. "The wigs looked like hats in the pictures online, but in person, you can tell they are made of human hair." He'd read about boys his age who went through an initiation rite lasting anywhere from a year and a half to three years. During their initiation, they would not cut their hair, and they couldn't have anything to do with girls. Not even their own mom. They had to eat strange foods which helped their hair grow, and they slept with a block under their neck to help their hair keep its shape. It looked awfully uncomfortable from the picture, but at the end of their initiation, when they reached adulthood, whatever that meant, the men would trim away the mass of hair they had grown. It would be given to the tribe's wigmaker, and they would weave it together and include various feathers and leaves and paints. Toby tried to imagine being separated from his mother and two sisters, not to mention not seeing any of the girls from school, for such a long time. It didn't seem to be a very good trade-off to give up your mom to get a fancy wig.

He turned his attention back to the field where another tribe began dancing. They wore grass skirts and had white paint across their foreheads and down their noses. A white headband wound around their head, holding a garland of greenery in place on their heads with feathers erupting from the front like a plume.

He flipped through the pages of his journal to identify the tribe and scribbled a few notes about their dance.

The next group brought the mood from jubilant celebration to solemn mourning. Their dance recreated the grieving ceremony following the death of a tribe member. They carried a long wooden pole, with what appeared to be a dead body wrapped up like a cocoon and hanging from the pole. The young men bearing the weight of their family member didn't seem to mind at all. One member of the tribe carried a sign which read "Dead Body," just in case the folks in the audience couldn't figure that out. The tribe dressed more somberly than all the others. They wore no bright, festive embellishments and had no choreographed dancing. They'd covered themselves in gray mud, with simple headdresses resembling a heavy veil stretching over their shoulders to the ground. Like a shroud, they wrapped themselves in this covering as they wailed over the loss of their loved one. Dark streaks of skin showed where their tears had cut a trail through the mud on their faces.

Toby had read about ancient and extinct traditions of some tribes which included eating members of their own family who had died. They had once believed it would give them the strength or abilities of their loved one or that the dead person would continue to live through them. He shivered and wrinkled his nose. It was strange and gross, but, like an onlooker drawn to gawk at a tragedy, the different rituals the tribes had once practiced captivated his imagination.

Miss Maryann's story about the glasman in the village and his accusations against Moia flashed through Toby's mind. He shivered again.

The sun hovered over the mountains, and the tribes continued to perform when Amy's dad motioned to the family it was time to head home. Ruth had fallen asleep on Slane, her head resting on his chest.

Amy reached to pick her up, but he waved her off and rose, holding her sister with one arm like a feather pillow. "I'll carry Ruth for you. No sense in waking her up." Amy nodded and shook out the blanket and stuffed it in the bilum bag she slung across her shoulder.

The whole family, plus Joaquin and Slane, followed her father as he threaded a path through the crowds to the street and their 4X4 parked next to others from the outpost. Slane handed his tiny burden off to her father.

"Thanks for letting us join you."

Her father shifted Ruth's weight in his arms. "No, thank you. Sorry, she just made herself comfortable. You must have been miserable with her dead weight resting on you all that time."

Slane shook his head and shrugged. "I never had a little sister. It was kind of nice."

His smile looked genuine, but his eyes looked sad. Staring into them, Amy suddenly felt awkward. She'd stumbled onto something much too personal. "Well, thanks again, and, um, good night." A blush crept into her cheeks, and she hoped the fading light would hide it.

Joaquin stepped in and hugged her, whispering in her ear, "Not a good idea, little sis. We're out of here in a couple of weeks."

"I don't know what you're talking about." She feigned confusion, but she got the message. Joaquin always saw through her. And he never failed to redirect her course when she steered toward trouble. She dropped a sisterly kiss on his cheek and added, "Thanks, big brother."

As she climbed into the Mule, her dad called out, "So we'll see you tomorrow night for dinner, right?"

Joaquin gave a thumbs up as they pulled away. Amy wrapped her arms around herself despite the warm evening. Excitement and apprehension battled inside her, but a smile lingered the whole ride home.

CHAPTER FIVE

Wara, Eastern Highlands Province, Papua New Guinea

Toby braced himself, determined not to let fear get the better of him this time. He'd conjured a story about Miss Maryann needing a strong young man to help with her garden as an excuse so he could handle the next medicine delivery. It wasn't a lie. She had said exactly that, and he had willingly volunteered. Of course, his volunteer mission had resulted in his parents insisting Brandon help as well. In their words, "two strong young men are better than one." And they'd sent Bublé along to keep them out of trouble.

He wanted to get a better look inside the glasman's hut. But now he had to escape his brother for a few minutes to explore. He stood and stretched his back. They'd been pulling weeds from among the small plot of strawberries, kaukau, and other vegetables all morning, and he wondered if his adventure was worth all the extra work. Brandon glared at him, apparently still sore over being directed to babysit.

"I'll be back in a minute. I need to use the liklik haus." He headed around the side of the missionary's home toward the spot where woven grass walls guarded the privacy of a hole in the ground covered by a plank of wood. It always made him grateful for their indoor plumbing when he had to use Miss Maryann's outhouse, but today it was just a ruse.

As soon as he escaped his brother's line of sight, he ducked past several huts toward the one where the glasman lived. Toby peeked through the branches forming the wall of the hut and saw the glasman, his bare chest painted with strange markings, sitting cross-legged by a smoldering fire. His beard reached to his gut, and he chanted over the skull of a pig in a language Toby didn't recognize. Yellowed seashells rested in the eye sockets of the pig, and the old man waved a handful of leaves over the fire and then brushed them over the skull. His voice carried a weird, raspy sound in the back of his throat.

Branches joined together with vines and covered with leafy palm fronds to deflect most of the rain formed the small hut. Inside, skulls like the one Toby had found in the woods perched on a wide branch which ran the width of the hut.

A young man from the village entered the hut and spoke to the man in a language Toby didn't understand. The glasman replied, and the villager pointed toward his gut, grimacing in pain. The bearded elder motioned for him to sit on the other side of the fire. The glasman continued his ritual, this time brushing the smoking leaves over the man as well as the pig skull. His chanting grew more feverish, and his motions gained a rhythm of their own. Toby held his breath, mesmerized by the display, his curiosity growing. With a shout, the painted man jabbed his hand toward the other man's gut and jerked it back, opening his palm to show him a small stone. The man immediately rose, almost dancing with joy. Obviously, whatever the glasman had done had worked.

Toby looked at the man's gut, but saw no evidence the glasman had touched him. Had he really pulled the stone out of the man somehow? Or was it like the magician he'd seen as a kid—the one whose rabbit snuck out of the hat when the magician wasn't looking?

He recoiled, taking a deep breath to calm his racing heart and told himself the whole thing must be fake, just like that magician. Bublé bounded up to him, sniffing and letting out a yip before Toby could shush him.

He leaned in to peer once more through the opening among the branches to find two piercing black eyes staring back inches away. The glasman had seen him!

Toby turned and ran as fast as he could back to Maryann's home, hating his fear, but not able to smother it. His breath came in quick gasps as he rounded the corner and collided with his brother.

"Whoa! Little dude, what's your hurry?" His brother laughed at him. "You look like someone scared it right out of you! What took so long?"

Toby squinted at his brother and swung a fist, but Brandon caught it and held him at arm's length. Toby was bigger and heavier, but Brandon had the strength and speed of an athlete as his advantage.

"Boys!" Miss Maryann's voice caused them both to drop their hands to their sides. She didn't miss the opportunity to remind them they should love and look out for one another rather than bicker and fight. When she wrapped up the lecture, she added one last admonishment as she pointed toward the mountain peak. "Now, you see those clouds coming over the mountain? We're fixin' to get a heavy rain. You'd both better skedaddle back home before it hits. The path will be treacherous in a storm."

Toby and Brandon glanced at the black clouds and nodded. They both took off at a jog down the footpath with Bublé loping along with them. They'd been caught in the rain before, and they didn't care to repeat the experience.

Halfway home, the sky opened up, and a torrential rainstorm began. The drops felt like pebbles pelting Toby from the sky. Rain fogged his glasses, limiting his visibility to only a few feet ahead. After just a few minutes, parts of the path sank like a bog, and the rest grew slippery, making running impossible. He slowed to a walk, but the mud sucked at his shoes, impeding his progress. Brandon urged him to move faster, but he couldn't go any faster. Even the dog struggled to keep moving.

When they reached the first bridge, Bublé ran ahead and howled at them to follow. Toby balked. "We shouldn't cross the bridge in this rain. My shoes are muddy and slippery."

"We've got to, Toby. It'll be okay. Just hold on to the ropes as you cross it."

Brandon went first, edging his way across to the mid-point where the first bridge ended on an island in the midst of the gorge.

"Come on, Toby!" He shouted over the pouring rain. "You can do it!" The dog joined in the chorus.

Toby edged out onto the bridge, clinging to the rope railing like a lifeline. In truth, it was. His feet had no traction on the slippery surface. He barely lifted them, shuffling along while his arms did most of the work. He was glad his rain-streaked glasses hid the view of the rocks below. When he reached the middle, he gave his brother the first hug they'd exchanged in a very long time.

Emboldened, Toby followed his brother closely as they crossed the second bridge. They'd reached the center of the bridge when he heard the distant rumble. It sounded almost like thunder, but closer. The roar didn't pause as thunder would, but continued, growing in volume, echoing through the gorge. Bublé's howls from the bank turned to urgent barking. The bridge swayed, and Toby almost lost his footing.

"Brandon, stop it! It's not funny!" He shouted over the din, thinking his brother was shaking the bridge.

"It's not me, Toby! I think it's an earthquake. Hold on to the rope."

As if he weren't already holding on as tight as possible, Toby clenched even tighter.

He looked upriver and glimpsed a boulder through a clear streak in his glasses as it dislodged near the top of the gorge and tumbled down, knocking trees and other rocks loose as it fell. Within seconds, one stone became a wall of mud and rocks and trees.

Brandon grabbed his hand, and they ran the last few strides to reach the other side. Bublé greeted him with a slobbery kiss and then raced ahead of them as if pursued by a vicious beast. The hill on this side of the gorge rose gently, but their muddy shoes still made it perilous. Keeping up with the dog was impossible. They climbed several feet and then slid back, then climbed again. They reached the crest and started down the slope toward the institute. Bublé, a hundred yards ahead, raced back toward them, barking and urging them on.

Toby panted from the effort, but relief flooded his heart as the roofs of the homes at the institute came into view and then, further down the valley, the village of Haedi, which lent its name to the outpost.

They'd escaped the ravine, but the sense of relief didn't last. A distant rumble pulled Toby's gaze toward the mountain, which overshadowed the path home. The sparse trees along the slope raced downhill, unfurling a bronzed carpet behind them.

The roar grew deafening, but terror froze his feet in place.

Brandon grabbed his arm and screamed, but his words were lost in the roar. Ignoring the slippery mud and their exhaustion, they ran as fast as they could. Bublé led the way, barking at them like a drill sergeant with recalcitrant recruits.

Toby's legs and lungs burned from the effort, but fear pushed adrenaline into his veins and kept him going. His brother grabbed his arm and pulled him off the path and across the green grass. They ran parallel to the wall of debris moving closer on their right.

"We need to run away from it!" He shouted above the roar.

Brandon shook his head and pointed to a small rise where Bublé waited, howling for them to follow. They'd never outrun the landslide. They'd have to reach the mound, or the mud and trees would swallow them up. The roaring beast inched closer every moment as Brandon dragged him up the incline.

Toby's foot caught on a root and sent him face first into the grass, jerking his hand from his brother's grasp. Before he could regain his footing, Bublé latched onto his collar and dragged him up the hill, his face smearing through the grass. They reached the summit of the small ridge seconds before the wall of mud, trees, and everything in its path swept past only feet below.

Toby rolled onto his back and sat up. Taking his glasses off, he tried to find a clean spot on his shirt to wipe them but settled for letting the rain rinse the grime away. He brushed at the clay and grass covering his chest as Bublé tried to help by bathing his face with his tongue. His brother collapsed beside him, and they watched in horror. A river a hundred yards wide opened up in the green hillside and drew everything it encountered down with it. The roar finally ended as the slide oozed to a stop in the valley below.

Bublé licked Toby's hand, and he buried his face in the coarse fur to hide his tears. A river of sludge lay between them and their home. The thatched roofs of the village had vanished. And just as quickly as they'd appeared, the clouds parted, and the sun shone as if it had never abandoned them.

Haedi Village

Amy focused on her new plan for serving as she hurried toward Haedi. First, she would visit the village to see if she might help Moia or any of the other mothers with young children.

Dark clouds hovered over the mountains, casting shadows of cobalt, but mid-afternoon sunshine lit up the valley. The path meandered up over a ridge and then downhill to where Laila's tiny, thatched-roof home sat with a few dozen others nestled between two ridges. The single room would fit within Amy's living room, but it housed Laila, her mother, her younger brother Rayz, and her six-month-old baby sister, Isa.

With limited indoor space, mostly used for cooking and sleeping, they spent much of their day outdoors. Amy found Laila sitting cross-legged on the ground in front of their home, creating a brightly colored bilum and talking with a young man who knelt beside her. He looked up and scowled when he saw Amy approaching.

Moia poked her head out and spied the young man. She shooed him away like a pesky varmint, swinging her arms and shouting at him in words Amy didn't understand until he fled.

She squatted beside her friend and watched Laila's nimble fingers at work. "Who was he?" Amy said in Tok Pisin, eager to practice her language skills.

"His name is Nizax. He lives in Wara. I was going to be his wife. . .before."

Amy cast a glance at his retreating back and remembered her parents' hushed conversations about the attack that had brought Moia's family to Haedi.

Laila continued, "He found us here. He said I must come back to Wara and be his wife. My father agreed to the marriage before he died, when we lived in Wara, but now my mother is changing her mind about many things. She says I would not be safe in Wara now." She spoke of marriage and their flight from Wara for their lives in a casual tone, but fear lurked in her eyes. The kind of fear one grows numb to because it is a constant presence, like living in the shadow of a volcano.

Amy tried to hide her shock. Contemplating marriage at such a young age seemed so strange, but she knew girls had been married off to pay debts or gain property at much younger ages. Laila passed her a length of the yarn and showed her how to twist and loop it to weave the fabric. She took the twine and tried several times to follow her friend's guidance but ended up with a knotted ball each time. Her friend patiently pulled the knots out and showed her again.

"Do you want to marry him? I mean, do you love him?"

Laila frowned at her. "It is not for me to want or not. He can take care of me and my family."

Amy sat in stunned silence, trying to get the yarn to cooperate. After the third time, she pulled the knots loose herself and laid the twine aside.

"What will happen now that he found you and your family here?"

"I don't know." Laila looked down, and Amy wondered if the moments before they escaped the mob still haunted her. Her fingers returned to their task, flying over the yarn even without her attention.

The ground underneath them trembled, and the thatched roof on the hut rustled with the movement. It lasted only a moment. An ominous stillness followed, broken suddenly by the call of birds clamoring toward the sky.

Laila's mother peered out of the hut, taking in the village and the two girls before returning to her tasks. Though not common, several earthquakes had rocked the Haedi Outpost with no major damage since Amy and her family moved to Papua New Guinea.

A muffled thunder echoed through the valley, but the sky remained clear overhead. The only clouds in sight poured rain on the mountains in the distance. The roar continued and grew louder, and Amy scanned the sky for a plane but saw nothing.

Laila looked toward the hillside behind Amy, and her eyes grew wide. Then, she jumped up and grabbed Amy's hand and pulled her to her feet, pointing to the monster behind them.

A swath of russet cut into the teal hillside. Like a road being built at lightning speed. It grew by the moment and headed toward the village.

Laila yelled at her above the growing tumult, but Amy couldn't make out the words.

"We have to get out of the path!" Amy pointed away from the coming landslide, but Laila pulled back.

"Mami!" Her mother appeared at the door, holding Isa on one hip and Rayz on the other. The landslide had reached halfway down the mountain and closed in on the village. Amy pulled the baby from Moia's arms so she could wrangle Rayz, and they fled the wall of debris racing toward them.

As they neared the top of the rise, the roar eased until Amy heard only her own ragged breathing. The land grew eerily quiet, and she wondered if every living thing had been wiped out by the river of mud and trees and rocks. She collapsed on her backside on the ground, still cradling Isa. Laila fell on all fours beside her, breathing hard.

The land awakened as if from a long nap. Birds called to their mates. Insects resumed their chirping. Laila's baby sister began to cry for her mother. Amy searched the area but didn't see Moia anywhere.

"Laila, where is your mother? She was right behind us."

Laila pushed herself to her feet and cried out in Tok Pisin, "Mami! Yu stap we?"

Amy's heart raced as she wondered what to do. The baby's wails grew louder.

Laila ran toward the village, calling for her mother in a voice increasing in panic with each echo.

Below, the landslide had buried the village. The flow of debris stopped when it reached the base of the valley where the ground began to rise toward the next ridge. Only a few trees dotted the hill Amy and Laila had ascended, and Amy checked each one for Laila's mother. Where did she go? What if she stumbled? They wouldn't have heard her cry over the ruckus. What if the slide had buried Moia and Rayz in the rubble? Laila had lost her father and almost lost her mother, and now she had lost everything.

The climb down underscored the miracle of their survival. The uneven hillside exposed a million spots where one wrong turn might twist an ankle or snap a bone. They'd raced up the incline as if it were smooth and even. It seemed like their feet had never touched the rough terrain.

The river of mud and debris had claimed the entire village, with no sign of Laila's mother anywhere.

Laila called again and again, first for her mother, then for her little brother.

Amy stilled her. "Hush. Let's listen for a moment in case they are calling for us."

In the silence, they heard the tiny whisper, little more than a moan. Laila's brother, Rayz, clung to the trunk of a tree submerged several feet in mud. Buried up to his knees, the mud coated his body, camouflaging him the same color as the landscape His thin arms embraced the tree as though it alone had kept him from being swept away.

Amy nestled the baby in the bilum bag and slung it on her back. They began scraping away the mud encasing the boy's bare feet and legs up to his knee. What they uncovered sent a cold chill down Amy's spine.

The brown hand of Laila's mother gripped the boy's ankle. He hadn't been able to pull his leg free of her grip. Amy glanced at Laila and met eyes filled with fledgling hope. Could her mother still be alive? How long had it been since the flow stopped? Could she breathe at all?

Laila dug furiously with both hands, trying to reach her mother in time. Amy knelt beside her in the mire and pulled debris out of the mud and tossed it aside.

The first hint of life came as they released Moia's fingers from Rayz's ankle, and she clenched her daughter's hand, silently begging her not to let go. Amy lifted the boy onto solid ground and settled the baby in his arms so she could work faster.

Tears flowed as Amy peeled Moia's fingers from Laila's hand so they could continue to dig. Once freed, Moia's hand flailed, grabbing at anything within reach. It seemed like hours but must have been less than a minute before they reached the top of her head. Laila scooped the mud away and lifted her mother's face. Moia raised her head. Her muddy lips praised God and gave thanks to them in Tok Pisin. She had curled herself into a tight ball, one arm wrapped around her knees while the other had gripped the boy's ankle as the mud swept over them. The small air pocket she created gave her the precious moments needed for them to reach her.

It took an hour to scrape away enough of the mud to free her body. As they continued to work, Amy pulled on a small branch jutting out of the mud. Moia let out a wail of pain.

The piece of wood had pierced her leg. Fearful of causing any further damage, Amy worked carefully around the debris until they freed Moia. Amy and Laila cradled her between them and moved her further up the hill. As Amy examined the wound, Moia moaned in pain, her hands twitching and trying to grasp the dagger in her leg.

The six-inch-long stick, perhaps an inch in diameter, had pierced her left thigh midway between buttock and knee. No doubt she would need stitches upon its removal, but more importantly, had it hit an artery? Amy learned in scouts that yanking it could cause her to bleed out in minutes. This situation far surpassed her lessons in first aid. She fashioned a tourniquet from her belt and hoped it would control the bleeding until help arrived.

A handful of villagers, those who had been outside working and seen the landslide coming, gathered near the edge of the mud. Some searched for evidence of survivors while others wept and lamented, too overwhelmed by their own grief to help. The villagers needed men and equipment to dig out any survivors, and Moia needed medical care.

"I'll run get help. You stay with her. Whatever you do, don't let her pull the branch out."

Laila nodded as she rocked her little brother and shushed the baby. "Please hurry."

Kopí Plantation

As Slane followed Joaquin down the row of coffee bushes, picking coffee cherries and dropping them into a bucket, the ground under his feet shuddered. In the distance, thunder rolled on and on.

"Was that an earthquake?" Slane had survived one earthquake during his time in South America, and he never wanted to relive the experience.

"Yes, but the noise following it? It was different." Joaquin paused as he dumped a handful of cherries into the bucket. "We should check on my aunt and uncle." They picked up the half-filled buckets and hurried back to Kopi.

Carlos met them in his Land Cruiser before they reached the house, his expression grim.

"The earthquake triggered a mudslide. Samson

just came from Haedi. The village is buried. Dump the coffee out; we might need those buckets and as many as we can carry."

They dumped the fruit of their labor on the ground, and Joaquin collected a dozen more buckets before they climbed in the cruiser. The road to Goroka had been bumpy, but with Carlos racing to save lives, they practically bounced over the potholes and ruts.

Slane braced himself as they rounded a tight curve, and Carlos slammed on the brakes, sending the cruiser sliding sideways on the wet pavement. They climbed out and stood gawking at the remains of the road. The cruiser stopped a foot away from a steep drop where the mudslide had obliterated the roadway, leaving a ten-foot deep and hundred-yard wide chasm. The flow of mud and debris separated them from the village with no way around it.

Carlos kicked a loose piece of asphalt and paced back and forth before he turned back to them. "We'll have to get the chopper. Let's go."

Carlos sped back over the road even faster than before. Slane held tight to the front seat as potholes pitched him high, and he ducked his head to keep from hitting it on the headliner. In no time, they arrived at the plantation and hopped aboard the chopper. Airborne, they skimmed over the treetops and searched for a spot to set down.

A bare hill fifty yards north of the village provided the best opportunity. As they touched down, Joaquin pointed out a woman and three children huddled under a tree.

Carlos shouted into their headphones, "Get the woman and kids onboard. I'll take them to the clinic at the outpost and then come back to help." Slane followed Joaquin down the steep hill to where the woman sat, cradling a baby with a small boy curled up beside her and a teenaged girl waving them over. The girl pointed to her mother's leg where a piece of wood, caked with mud and blood, protruded from her thigh. Slane's stomach lurched, and he was glad they'd missed lunch.

He and Joaquin lifted the woman gently and carried her to the helicopter. She moaned each time the rough terrain jostled her. They settled her in the back of the copter and strapped her and the children in with the teenager holding her baby sister.

Carlos shouted over the sound of the engine, "You two, take the buckets and head down to the village and start digging."

Slane's memory conjured images of the earthquake in Peru, and he fought a sense of panic over what they would find in the village.

The two of them hiked back down the hill until they reached the place where the mud cascaded like a lava flow through the hollow.

Following the edge of the mudflow to where the village once stood, they began to search for any signs of life.

Several men from the village frantically dug through the mud with their hands, picking up smaller stones and rolling larger ones away. Slane and Joaquin passed out the buckets and began to scoop the mud and haul it into the woods to dump it.

Digging through the muck made Slane's back ache and his shirt stick to his skin despite the cool, dry air at this elevation. Still, he kept it on even after others left theirs hanging on a nearby bush. His gaze fell on one of the men from the village who bore tiny, raised scars all over his back, like the pattern of a crocodile's scales. Slane flinched, his own back sensing the pain of each scar.

"That is Iatmul." Joaquin whispered. "He is from a tribe along the Sepik River. As part of their ritual for initiating young boys into manhood, they receive these markings, cuts in the flesh made to resemble a crocodile, which is a powerful symbol to their tribe." Slane glanced away, sensing his friend's disapproval of his gawking, but unwilling to explain. Joaquin didn't know what he'd been through. Slane understood all too well the pain of being forever marked by membership in a group.

Three men worked together to heft large rocks out of the way while Slane used the buckets to clear the mud left behind. The sludge weighed more than he expected. The villagers worked with surprising speed. Even after all the hard labor onboard the ship, the unaccustomed motion left his shoulders and pecs burning.

His stomach complained with a loud growl about how long it had been since breakfast. Lunchtime had passed before they even began, and no one had stopped to eat. Joaquin had warned him they didn't always eat lunch but made dinner the primary meal of the day. How did they work so hard without a break or a meal?

The image of the woman on the hill clinging to life flashed through his mind. He glanced at the other men, continuing to work quickly. These men dug and searched for their families. The thought spurred him on.

One of the villagers stopped to stuff a wad of green leaves, wrapped around a nut and coated with a white powder, in his mouth. He chewed on it and spit a stream of red juice through his teeth into the mud. He met Slane's stare and offered to share.

Thinking this must be some local variety of food, Slane accepted. The man demonstrated how to wrap the betel leaves around the areca nut and coat it with lime and then showed him how to put it between his cheek and his teeth to chew it.

The peppery taste burned and gave him a jolt of energy. He scooped up mud and hauled it off and hurried back. His heart raced, and he worked with lightning speed. Joaquin shook his head and smirked.

"It's a stimulant, like the coca leaves chewed in South America. Very addictive, and not so good for your teeth." He pointed to the one who had given it, and the man grinned, revealing decayed, blood-red teeth.

Slane frowned and spit out the nasty mess as soon as his gracious new friend turned away.

On the road to Haedi Outpost

Toby and Brandon stayed near the mudflow as Bublé led them down the side of the mountain. Brandon pointed toward the outpost. "I think if we follow the mudflow as far as the road, then we should be able to take the road back home."

But when they reached the road, they found only skid marks leading up to a ragged edge of asphalt, a steep drop off, and more mud. They stood at the edge of the asphalt and gazed out over the valley to see how far the landslide had reached.

Bublé yapped at them, complaining when they didn't heed his warning.

"It's ok, boy." Brandon ruffled the dog's ears and stepped closer, shielding his eyes from the late afternoon glare. But the dog barked again and latched onto Brandon's shorts as the stones beneath their feet rumbled. The asphalt under his brother's feet cracked. Toby dove sideways, tackling Brandon just before the ground gave way where he'd been standing. They landed hard and Brandon's breath exploded in Toby's face as his weight landed on his older brother's chest.

Bublé howled to say, "I told you so."

Toby rolled off Brandon and crawled away from the edge as his brother lay flat on his back, sucking in air.

"I promise," he rubbed a hand across his ribs and grimaced as he rolled to his side, "I will never call you little dude again."

Toby might have celebrated the victory if panic weren't rising in his chest, threatening to overwhelm and strangle him. "How are we going to get home? We can't hike all the way around the whole valley." He stared at the wide expanse of destruction. In answer, the sound of a helicopter reverberated off the mountains and filled the valley.

"It's Carlos!" Toby shaded his eyes against the sun. He jumped to his feet and waved and hollered. Bublé joined the chorus like he understood the goal. Brandon even shouted and waved his arms a few times, but Carlos didn't seem to see them. The chopper emerged from a hollow beyond a rise on the other side of the mud and angled toward the outpost.

"Now what?" Toby crumpled cross-legged onto the asphalt, dejected,. The dog licked at his hands, but Toby shoved his head away.

"Not now, Bublé."

"Don't worry, Toby. Carlos must be helping transport people who are hurt. He'll be back. We need to watch for him to come back and find a way to get his attention."

His brother's encouragement caught him off guard, but he nodded in silence.

"We need to be ready when he's headed back toward the village." Brandon picked up a long stick and began poking around the edge of the mud and through the grass nearby. "Help me search for a bottle or a piece of broken glass. We can use it to reflect the sunlight to catch his eye. Or maybe look for something we can light a signal fire with."

Toby pushed himself off the wet pavement and joined the search. Thirty minutes went by before he stopped and began to laugh. His brother straightened up from where he had been digging in the mud and asked, "What's so funny?"

Toby took off his glasses and held them up, still laughing. "We have glass right here. It's like when mom is searching for her glasses, and she's wearing them."

CHAPTER SIX

Haedi Outpost

Amy raced through the long grass toward the outpost a mile up the mountain from the village which shared its name. The village now buried by the landslide.

"Help! We need help!" She shouted as she approached the guard at the gate.

Mr. Dan emerged from the guard station.

"What happened?" He called out as he ran to meet her.

"Landslide." Winded, she didn't have enough breath to utter a complete sentence. "Village." She pointed in the direction of the village as she held her side and tried to catch her breath. "Buried."

He turned and ran back toward the station. He hopped in the ancient Volkswagen camper and pulled it around the guard station to meet her. Flinging the door, he shouted, "Hop in!"

Amy climbed in the passenger seat, and he raced down the dirt road, horn blaring. Families poured out of their homes, and he slowed down enough to shout through his open window, "Landslide at Haedi! Meet at the gate." They reacted immediately, running to gather tools and first aid kits.

When Mr. Dan had completed a circuit of the small community, he returned to the gate where a crowd assembled, armed with supplies. As Amy's pulse eased, the reality of what she had witnessed set in. Her hands shook, and the trembling soon spread to her arms and legs. Despite the warmth of the sun, her teeth chattered so hard she wondered if they would break. She climbed out of the van but kept one hand on the door. The adrenaline which had pumped through her veins as she raced up the mountain now jumbled her thoughts and weakened her knees.

With a crowd of residents surrounding her and more running toward the gate, Mr. Dan hollered for quiet and turned to her.

"Tell everybody what you saw."

Amy opened and closed her mouth, but no words came out. He wanted her to explain. But tremors possessed her body, making speech impossible. His hands gripped her shoulders and gave a quick shake, snapping her to attention.

"Amy, we need to know exactly what happened so we can help those in the village." His voice sounded hard as granite.

"Th-there was a l-l-landslide. Th-the village is b-b-buried." Audible gasps filled the silence for the space of a heartbeat before folks sprang into action. Some returned to their homes to retrieve more equipment or family members. Several set out right away, running toward the village to offer help.

Amy's mother and father elbowed their way through the crowd around her.

"Are you hurt?" Her mother hugged her close and then held her at arm's length, surveying her for any damage.

"I-I'm fine. But L-laila's mom is h-hurt. She needs a d-d-doctor."

"Where is she?" Her father waved over one of the volunteers who helped at the medical clinic.

"She's under a t-tree on the hill just this s-s-side of the village."

Her mother rubbed her hands up and down

Amy's arms. "Are you sure you are all right? You're white as a sheet and cold as ice."

"I-I'm ok-kay." But her knees buckled like someone had knocked them out from under her. Her mother's arms clenched around her, and her view of the mountains spun, then tilted as her mother stumbled. Her father's strong arms scooped her up as the blue skies faded to black.

Amy awoke to the feel of the grass under her, and the scent of her father's shirt as he cradled her head in his lap.

"Amy."

Her eyelids fluttered. Her mother knelt beside her and held Amy's wrist between a thumb and two fingers, taking her pulse. Remembrance dawned, and she tried to sit up. The effort made her dizzy, and she held her head and rested it on her father's chest.

"What happened?"

"You fainted. You're in shock, honey." Her mother patted her hand in a gesture too small for the magnitude of the crisis. If you faced a life-threatening emergency, you'd want her mom as your nurse — cool and calm in the face of trauma. But if you needed a shoulder to cry on over a minor injury, you should look elsewhere.

"But. . .Laila. Her mother. Are they okay?" Her mom's eyes communicated a silent message with her dad. Even her nurse's façade didn't hide the worry as her brows drew tight, and she glanced away.

"Everyone who can has gone to help. I'm sure they will be fine. We'll do everything we can." Her father exchanged another worried look with her mom.

"I'll join them as soon as I can."

What weren't they telling her?

She sat up, desperate to convince them she felt okay. "I'm fine, Dad. Please, please, will you go make sure Laila and her family are safe?" She tried in vain to hold back the tears.

"I will." His eyes locked with her mother's, and Amy perceived the slightest nod of assent for him to tell all. He rested one large hand over her smaller one. "First, I have to find your brothers. They went to Wara today and haven't returned yet."

Her breath caught in her throat and threatened to choke her. What if Brandon and Toby were on the road when the landslide hit? She pulled away and forced herself to stand, only swaying a tiny bit. "You've got to go. I'm fine." The sound of Carlos's helicopter interrupted her plea.

They hurried to the field where the helicopter settled on the grass near the clinic. Her mom kept one arm around Amy's waist in case she fainted again. At the sight of Laila emerging from the chopper, she almost did. Her friend climbed out and swung the bilum with her baby sister on her back as she helped her little brother take the long step down from the helicopter. Several volunteers rushed out of the clinic and helped Carlos lift Laila's mother gently out of the seat and onto a litter. Laila hovered alongside, holding her mother's hand in one hand and her little brother's in the other.

Amy's father ran to the pilot's side and grabbed his arm. "Carlos, my boys are out there. They went to Wara this morning, and they aren't back yet."

Carlos nodded. "We'll scan the trail on our way back to the village." Her dad hopped in beside Carlos, and Amy watched as they lifted off and angled toward the mountains.

On the road to Haedi Outpost

Toby heard the chopper first. "Here he comes!" He pulled off his glasses and began angling them to catch the sunlight and reflect it at the helicopter.

Within a few seconds, the trajectory of the chopper skewed toward them. They jumped up and down, waving their arms to be sure Carlos saw them. As he descended, they moved out of the way, pulling the dog along with them to give Carlos space to land on the asphalt near the slide.

The rotor slowed, and they hunched over and ran to climb aboard. Toby grabbed his dad in an awkward hug as he settled into his seat. Brandon whistled, and Bublè cast an anxious look around before running and jumping onto his lap. Carlos handed them the headphones, and Toby heard his voice in the built-in speaker. "Ready for take-off? Good!" He lifted off even as they fumbled for the seatbelts.

Carlos ascended a hundred feet, hovering over the debris field as he traveled downstream. The four scanned the mud for any movement or life. Then Carlos landed on a hill on the other side.

When they set down, Samson and Iatmul met them with a small child. Samson explained that they'd pulled him from a hut on the edge of the village. Only the hut's location on the periphery of the village had saved the boy, but everyone else in his family had been lost. The bodies pulled from the mud lay in a neat row, and Toby silently thanked God for his empty stomach as it lurched into his throat.

Carlos waved the boys out of the helicopter. "Sorry, boys, I need the space to carry the injured back to the institute. You can make it back on foot from here after you've helped search for any survivors."

"Thanks for the lift." Toby's dad clapped a hand on Carlos's shoulder. "Let Ellen and Amy know the boys are fine and they're with me, would you?"

Carlos gave a thumbs up and a nod in reply.

Toby, Brandon, and their father exited the chopper with Bublè close behind as Samson climbed in with the boy in his arms.

His dad wrapped an arm around each of them, pulling them close, and Toby thought he might be crying.

"Praise the Lord, you're both alright. Carlos told me he'd find you, but flying over the slide looking for any sign of you—" His voice broke, and he cleared his throat.

Toby pulled back, shifting uncomfortably as he felt a dozen pairs of eyes on them.

"We're fine, Dad. Really."

His dad nodded and released them. "I know. I'm just so thankful we found you." Bublé jumped on him, begging for a greeting of his own, and their dad ruffled the tawny ears a few times.

The helicopter rose from the hill, stirring up debris in a whirlwind around them. Toby stumbled, trying to keep up with his father and brother as they hurried down the slope to where friends from the institute had joined the men from the village. The task seemed impossible. They used buckets and shovels and their bare hands to dig into the mud and pull out whatever they found. His mind returned to the image of the bodies lined up in a row, and he squelched the urge to vomit.

Toby spied the friend of Joaquin's, Slane, who they had met at the singsing. Whenever Joaquin visited, he always brought stories of his adventures at sea, but maybe this newcomer had his own tales. Toby locked away the overwhelming picture of death and sought instead the distraction of drama. He worked his way closer to Slane and began adding debris to the bucket beside him.

Slane scooped up mud and sticks and rocks and loaded the five-gallon bucket. He towered a head taller than Toby and scooped up twice as much with each shovelful. Toby worked in silence for a few minutes before curiosity got the best of him. "So you work on the ship with Joaquin?"

The tall newcomer nodded but kept silent, his lips pressed in a grim line. Toby persisted. "What is it like?"

Slane shrugged, and the silence stretched for a long, awkward moment before he answered. "It's hard work. And kind of lonely sometimes. And when all you can see everywhere you look is water, it's pretty intense." He jerked his head toward Toby, slinging the hair out of his eyes. "Why? Do you want to join us?" He laughed, and Toby bristled.

"What's so funny about that?"

"Sorry, I didn't mean it was funny exactly. But why would you want to give up all this for a life at sea?" He scanned the carnage surrounding them and adjusted his comment. "Well, I don't mean this." He swung his arms wide to take in all the chaos. "But you have a family, a home. Why would you leave them behind?"

Toby shrugged. He pondered Slane's words as they continued the grim work of searching for survivors. It got him thinking differently about his desire for excitement. Whatever he might be searching for, danger had certainly found him.

Slane focused on a small section of the debris at a time, tossing the stones and branches aside, and then scooping out mud with both hands to fill the bucket. The teenaged boy hefting rocks beside him had grown quiet, thankfully. He didn't need a million questions. He braced himself for what they might find. Images of death that he hadn't entertained in two months taunted him.

Still, the silence fed a tension lodged between his shoulder blades like a knife. His stomach emitted a loud growl, slicing through the dread, and the boy burst out laughing. Slane had given up on lunch after his experience with chewing betel nut, but his stomach still ached.

"It sounded like an alien was about to explode from your gut." The kid reached in the bag slung over his shoulder and offered Slane a handful of Snax Biscuits. Skeptical after his last encounter with PNG generosity, he hesitated a moment, but his hunger overruled his better judgment. He wiped his mud-caked hands on his pants and accepted the offering. The biscuits tasted a lot better than betel nut, that was for sure. Bland, but they did silence the hunger pangs.

The boy looked to be about fourteen, but big for his age. He had the awkward gait of a kid who had grown too big too fast and hadn't quite learned how to operate his large frame. He tucked his chin as he handed Slane a worn-out soda bottle, refilled with water, to wash the crackers down. Slane recognized the mix of curiosity, fear, and stubbornness he had at the same age. Poor kid.

"What's your name?"

The boy glanced up and then tucked his head again before mumbling, "Toby."

"You're Amy's brother, right?" He stuffed the last biscuit in his mouth and stuck out his hand. The boy shook it, his hand muddy and clammy and easily as large as Slane's. "So, how long have you lived here?"

The boy shrugged and said, "About seven years."

"How do you like it?"

Toby warmed up. "It's pretty cool. I like living at the outpost, and Dad lets me take medicine up the mountain to a little village called Wara." He raised his chin as he described the responsibility he'd been given and pointed toward the mountainside even though the village lay over the mountain out of view.

"I guess you'll be glad when we get this road cleared."

"Yeah, my brother and I were headed home from Wara when the mudslide happened. We ran up that hill." He pointed to a rise in the distance, an island rising above the flow of debris. "We have to take her next week's supply of medicine, and if we aren't able to get through, Ms. Maryann won't be able to help the people."

"So, you're kind of a hero, huh?"

"Nah, not really." But Slane caught the pride flashing in his eyes. "I do it because I get to hike way up the mountain, over this cool bridge." The boy's face clouded as he said it, working to convince himself rather than Slane. But he continued without a pause, "and sometimes I see super cool stuff along the way."

Slane smiled at his choice of words and played along. "What's the super coolest thing you've seen on your hikes up the mountain?"

Toby's face lit up. He glanced both ways. The other workers pulled a thatched roof intact from the debris, ignoring Toby.

"Once I found a bone." He leaned in closer and whispered, "A human bone."

Slane tried not to laugh at Toby's earnest secrecy. "How do you know it's a human bone?"

Toby appeared confused, as if the thought hadn't occurred. He glanced around again and slipped his hand in his pocket. He pulled his fist out and uncurled his fingers. A small reddish-brown segment of bone rested in his sweaty palm. "See? It's a finger bone, a phalanx."

Slane picked up the piece and studied it. He'd seen some grisly sights, especially running with Gerardo's gang, but he'd never seen a human bone. It certainly resembled one. Still, it might be from another mammal. "How can you be sure it isn't from an ape or a monkey or something?"

Toby guffawed and shook his head. A few nearby heads turned their way. He leaned in close again and whispered. "Primates don't live in PNG, except humans." His tone indicated Slane should have known this. "Besides, I went back to where I discovered it, and I found the skull, too. I think the glasman had something to do with it. The skull looked just like the ones I saw in the glasman's hut when I watched him chanting and performing some sort of weird ritual. Then a man from the village came in and the glasman reached inside him and pulled out a stone. The glasman turned and stared right at me through the crack. It was so creepy." But the kid grinned like creepy was a good thing.

A chill ran up Slane's spine despite the sweat coating his body. "Maybe you should tell someone about this. It might be dangerous."

"No, I'm going to figure out where it came from myself."

"That's definitely not a good idea, Toby." He'd seen enough death to know to stay as far from this mystery as possible. "You don't know who might be behind it or what they're capable of."

"Why? You think you know this place better than me? I don't need anyone's help."

The words touched a place in Slane's heart as if he were listening to his younger self. How much trouble would he have spared himself if he had been willing to admit he needed help sometimes? Or if he'd had someone willing to offer him help? Instead, he always had to prove he was smart enough or tough enough to take on whatever came his way. He shook his head.

"Toby, we all need help sometimes. And it is really important to be able to see when you need to ask for help. Take it from me."

The boy's face hardened into a scowl. He shrugged and snatched the treasure out of Slane's palm, stuffing it in his pocket. "You'd better not tell anyone."

Slane held up his hands in surrender. "I won't, but you should." Toby shook his head and walked away.

CHAPTER SEVEN

Haedi Outpost

Amy stood beside Laila and bounced Isa gently as they visited with Moia. The tiny clinic, which usually treated minor injuries and expectant mothers, had been converted to a hospital ward. Makeshift beds for those awaiting transport to the hospital in Mount Hagen filled every inch of space.

Laila's mother laid on her right side with a hand curled under her head. Thick bandages wrapped around her leg where the injury had been cleaned and stitched up.

Amy's mother stopped at the foot of the cot to update them.

"She'll be airlifted to Mount Hagen for x-rays as soon as possible. We're concerned her femur might be fractured. Unfortunately, she will have to wait, perhaps a day, as several others more critical need transport. But I think she will be fine once it heals."

"Tenkyu Tenkyu tru Tenkyu tumas." Laila thanked Amy's mom.

"Nogat samting Maski." Her mother accepted the gratitude with casual ease. "You and your brother and sister can stay with us until your mom is well and your home is rebuilt." She turned to Amy, "Amy, get them set up to share the room with you and Ruth, and Rayz can bunk with your brothers."

She didn't wait for Amy to agree but hurried on to check on other patients. After Laila's mother nursed Isa, Amy and Laila left to let her rest. Laila snuggled the drowsy little one in her bilum bag and hung it on her back. Amy held Rayz's hand as they set out on the dirt road toward home. With the sun easing over the mountains, those who had gone to help in the village filed back through the gate. Amy paused, squinting into the twilight to search for the familiar silhouettes of her brothers. Carlos had sent word they were fine and helping out at the village, but she wanted to see for herself.

She recognized Joaquin and his gangly friend, Slane, as they came through the gate. Their weary shoulders told her they hadn't brought much good news despite their efforts. As they walked down the slope toward her, Slane seemed even taller than she remembered. His shirt stretched tight at the shoulders but hung loose at the waist and clung to him with the sweat from hard work. A shock of unruly brown hair hung over his eyes, and he pushed it back with the palm of his hand, oblivious to the grime clinging to his hands after hours of digging. His gaze met hers with an intensity that caused her face to flush. She turned toward Joaquin instead.

She started to greet him with her customary sisterly hug but thought better of it as she took in his mud-caked clothes.

"What? No hug for me?" He spread his arms wide and laughed as he used his thumb to deposit a smudge on her nose. She wrinkled her nose and wiped the dirt away. Her smile faded as she recalled their mission.

"Did you find other survivors?"

"We pulled thirteen people out of the debris." Joaquin crossed his arms as if it had grown cold. He cast his eyes at Laila and lowered his voice. "But only seven of them made it to the helicopter. We thought we might find Carlos here. He's our lift back to Kopí."

He elbowed his friend and seemed to try to lighten the mood. "Plus, we need food. This guy seems to think he needs more than betel nuts to keep him going."

She wrinkled her nose again and recoiled. "Disgusting, Joaquin. You did not give him betel nuts, did you?"

Joaquin smirked. "No, but I didn't warn him when Samson gave him some."

She balled up her fist and gave his shoulder a slug. "That's no way to treat a friend!"

"But your brother shared some of his snacks with me." Slane shrugged. "Where I'm from, lunch is the biggest meal of the day. Dinner is usually cold cuts, sliced bread, and cheese." He rubbed his stomach as it rumbled in response.

"That doesn't sound like a South American dinner. I thought you joined the Katie in Peru?" She didn't mean to interrogate him, but she couldn't figure out why his name sounded so familiar. And his intense scrutiny sent chill bumps down her arm with a sensation somewhere between fear and excitement. She'd turn the tables and put him under the microscope.

"I joined the crew in Peru, but I'm not Peruvian. I happened to be in Peru when I joined the crew. I'm originally from Czechia. The Czech Republic, to use its official name." He shifted his gaze, and she continued probing.

"Oh, yeah, I remember you mentioning that at the festival. Prague, right? How on earth did you get all the way from the middle of Europe to South America?" Even in the fading daylight, she saw his neck and face darken as his gaze turned toward the mountain. What was he hiding?

A muscle flexed in his jaw, and he responded, still

staring somewhere in the distance. "It's a long story." Apparently not one he wanted to share. He focused those piercing dark eyes back on her. "How on earth did you get all the way from America to Papua New Guinea?" He raised his eyebrows, daring her to continue her questioning.

She backed down and cut her eyes sideways. *Hmph.* She felt certain he hid more than just a handsome face behind that lock of hair. But still, he'd helped search for survivors and clear the road, and they needed a meal. She turned pointedly toward Joaquin, ignoring his friend for a moment.

"I think Carlos left a little while ago to airlift a couple of the serious injuries to Mount Hagen. He should be back before too long. I'm sure we have plenty if you'd like to join us for dinner."

Joaquin laughed and nodded. "Yes. We would love to." He emphasized the "we" a bit too much for her liking, but she knew her parents would never approve of her slighting a guest by limiting the invitation to her old friend.

She glanced up at the sound of the 4X4 coming through the gate. Two passengers and a dog hopped out as Mr. Dan pulled the gate closed for the evening, and the mule continued toward the clinic. Toby's unmistakable silhouette and Brandon's leaner frame approached as Bublé loped ahead of them. Without another word to Joaquin or his enigmatic friend, she dropped Rayz's hand and ran to meet her brothers.

They might annoy her ninety-nine percent of the time, but she'd never been so glad to see them. Mud or no mud, she hugged first one and then the other several times.

"Whoa! Enough already!" Toby hollered when he had had enough of her sisterly affection. Bublé jumped up and rested his paws on her waist, wanting a hug as well.

She blinked away tears and buried her eyes in his coat. Wiping her face, she pivoted toward home, holding her brothers' hands as she had when the three of them were little.

Joaquin and Slane followed behind them, and she felt those endless dark eyes on her every step of the way.

Slane's gaze never left the slight blonde with the attitude. Their conversation at the cultural festival had been friendly, but this exchange reminded him of the sparks that had flown between him and Mara.

A sick feeling settled in the pit of his stomach as he recalled how his last fiery encounter with Mara ended. He pressed his lips together and stuffed the guilt deep into his gut. He loathed the fool he'd been, but he'd learned a lot since then.

Venting his anger had accomplished nothing but suffering, mostly his own. It had also brought pain for those he cared about. Still, knowing how much anguish it caused hadn't given him the power to control it.

Snapping back to the present, Slane stopped short, nearly running into Amy's arm as she swept it toward her home. "Welcome. Make yourselves at home. You're welcome to use the bathroom to clean up before dinner."

The two brothers led the way inside, with Laila and Rayz behind. Joaquin and Slane followed, but Amy stopped Slane at the bottom step.

"I know you're hiding something, and I'm going

to find out what it is." She folded her arms across her chest and glared at him like a suspect on trial, daring him to argue. "Your name seems very familiar." Her eyes narrowed as she tried to see through his charade. His heart lurched. Could she know about his history? It seemed impossible.

He forced a casual shrug. Meeting her gaze, he forced himself to stand firm. Was he that easy to read? "There are other people with the same name." His voice sounded weak, the last syllable increasing in pitch, more of a question than a statement. How could this tiny girl unnerve him so?

She nodded slowly and pursed her lips, unconvinced. "I'm going to figure it out."

What did she suspect him of hiding? Truthfully, he had hidden plenty. From her. From Joaquin. From the captain. A tremor ran up his spine as he considered the consequences if they discovered the truth about him. He couldn't let that happen. Not even for a pretty girl.

She turned, and they continued up the stairs in silence, Slane growing more uncomfortable with every step. He hadn't asked to come with Joaquin. And he had worked hard without complaining.

Well, without complaining too much.

And now this girl acted like his name alone made him a criminal. She didn't know all the things he had done, yet she judged him guilty without any evidence. Tension built in his shoulders and arms, and he clenched his fists, arms stiff by his sides. Maybe the guilt he felt showed plainly for all to see.

Joaquin met him at the top of the steps, reaching out a hand and resting it on his shoulder with a squeeze. Amy went into the house, but Joaquin held Slane back for a moment.

"Remember what I told you at Duffy's? I said you seemed like you were fighting an invisible enemy. It looks to me like you're in one of those battles."

Slane frowned, but his eyes followed Amy through the window in the door.

"But she is not your enemy."

Joaquin was right.

He grappled with a foe much more fearsome than a seventeen-year-old girl.

"You're right," Slane admitted. Joaquin's warm hand on his shoulder invited him to say more, but fear kept him silent.

Their eyes met, and his friend smiled tightly and nodded. The small gesture sucked the fight right out of Slane. Joaquin saw his struggle and had his back. He accepted Slane regardless of whether he ever came clean about his past. Such unconditional acceptance made all the difference in the world. He had never had a friend quite like this before.

Amy couldn't place where she'd heard Slane's name before, but she knew she had. And something about his name stirred anxiety. She mentally scanned all the names of people she recalled, acquaintances from back home, people who had visited on mission trips, articles she'd read, but nothing clicked.

His face didn't seem familiar; she would have remembered meeting him. She would never have forgotten those dark eyes gazing out from under his unruly mane. The tangled-up feelings of attraction and angst intrigued her. She shook off the feeling as she prepared dinner and set the table.

Her parents returned just as they sat down.

"Thanks for handling dinner, sweetheart." Her mom dropped a kiss on her forehead on her way to clean up.

"How was Moia when you left?" Amy asked.

"She's doing well." Her mom appeared weary, and mud coated her dad's clothes and arms. The two of them disappeared into the tiny bathroom while Amy and the others prayed over the meal.

Joaquin broke the tense silence. "So, Amy, how is school going? You'll graduate soon, won't you?"

"In about six months. Brandon and I will finish high school at the same time." Joaquin continued with his casual questioning until conversation flowed. She had to admire him for working to repair the rift as diligently as he'd worked to dig out survivors at the village.

He pretended to whisper behind his hand to Slane, "This girl is a smart one. Graduating a year early." She saw the spark of respect and admiration in the stranger's eyes and hated the pride welling up. Why did she care so much about what this stranger thought of her?

"Have you decided where you will go to college?"

Joaquin's voice pulled her attention back to the conversation, and she let out a sigh.

"No. I've been researching some, but I'm not sure."

"Still planning to be a nurse and a veterinarian and a doctor?" He teased her with the list of occupations she had claimed at age ten.

"I think I've settled on being a doctor, if I can get through med school."

"I'm sure you will. You've never let anything stop you when you set your mind on it. Remember when you decided you would learn to play soccer just to best me at my own game?"

She laughed. Seeing her old friend again reminded her of happy days spent chasing a soccer ball in the sun and oblivious to the dangers in the world around them. Blissfully unaware that the mountain might come crashing down and wipe out a whole village in a matter of minutes.

The memory of the sound of debris pouring down the mountain and destroying everyone and everything in its path sent a shiver up her spine. Her stomach burned at the image of the stick protruding from Moia's leg, which flashed through her mind. She fought the impulse to retch. What if she didn't have what it takes to be a doctor? What if she couldn't stomach seeing gross injuries?

The conversation must have taken a turn she missed as her thoughts drifted. Joaquin now spoke with Laila about the village. Her eyes met Slane's and then darted away from his worried gaze.

Her parents returned as Laila recounted their trauma. "It happened so quickly. We ran as fast as we could, but we didn't have time to warn anyone." Her voice broke.

"It lasted only a few minutes. And it destroyed everything. Did you find any other survivors?" Fear suddenly filled her eyes. "Did you find Nizax?"

Amy recalled her last sight of Nizax just moments before the landslide as he walked away. If he had survived, wouldn't they have seen him? What if he escaped the landslide and returned to Wara with the news of where Moia and her family were hiding?

"Of fifty in the village, we've accounted for about a dozen." Joaquin covered Laila's hand with his own. "We didn't find him."

And just like that, the oppressive silence

returned.

CHAPTER EIGHT

Haedi Village

As the sun came up, Toby squeezed between his brother and dad in the 4X4 to ride to the village. *Well, to what had been the village.* The sun barely had peeked over the mountain when Slane and Joaquin arrived in the helicopter to help the growing rescue and recovery team.

Toby wished he hadn't told the stranger about his secret. But keeping secrets proved harder work than moving boulders, and he needed to share his secret with someone. He just hoped the new guy wouldn't tell his dad.

As they continued to dig through the mud and debris, Toby recognized remnants of the village in the debris. First, he found a woven bilum bag, and then a clay pot. He pulled out the branches and saplings used to construct one of the homes, a length of the liana still holding them together.

They worked as a team with Toby, Joaquin, and Slane shoveling mud and debris into buckets, and Brandon and Toby's dad hauling the buckets away to dump them. They stacked branches in a pile to be used once the rescue phase ended and the rebuilding began.

Toby's back ached from the effort of shoveling the wet, soupy mud. He stretched and turned to Brandon. "I'll fill one more bucket, but then can we switch places?"

"Okay." His brother laughed. "But I'm not sure hauling buckets of this sludge is any easier than shoveling it, Little Dude." Toby shrugged and returned to his shoveling. As he dug the shovel into the slop, it struck something solid. He aimed a little closer and jabbed the shovel into the mud again. Still, he met resistance. He scraped back the mud on the surface and almost retched at the sight of an arm. His shovel had dug into the flesh in two places, but no blood flowed from the wounds. The skin looked ashy gray instead of ebony. He swept away more mud to reveal the head and shoulders of a young man not much older than he.

That was it. He took two steps away and heaved his entire breakfast into the miry slush.

Brandon called his father over and pointed out the arm while he covered his mouth with his other hand. The greenish color of his face suggested he might follow Toby's lead.

Toby wiped his mouth and hovered nearby, clenching his aching stomach to keep it where it belonged.

His dad stared at the corpse, then closed his eyes for a moment, his lips moving in silent prayer. Finally, he gestured to the four younger men. "We need to get him out. His family will want to mourn him properly." Without another word, he dropped to his knees and began scraping the mud away gently with his hands.

The four of them scooped mud into the buckets and took turns hauling them away in silence until they uncovered the entire body. The man lay face down, arms stretched over his head like he'd been knocked off his feet by the torrent. With most of the mud scraped away, Toby's father and Slane pulled him out and rolled him over on the grass. Toby recognized him. He'd been coming to the church at the institute, but Toby didn't know his name.

Slane went to a distant place in his mind as they wrapped the man's body and loaded it on the chopper to be delivered to the clinic. Carlos explained that a makeshift morgue had been established where people might claim their loved one's remains, if any family remained. Slane nodded to convey he understood Joaquin's uncle, but inside, numbness blocked any feeling.

They had all grown somber as the real purpose of their work became painfully clear. For Slane, it felt like he dug to unearth the nightmare of his past. He moved a little farther downstream, away from the evidence of their discovery. But the teenaged boy followed him. The kid's persistence reminded Slane of himself, especially his angry brooding.

When they were out of hearing of Toby's father, Slane paused and leaned on the shovel. "So, have you told your father about what you've been doing yet?"

Toby folded his arms like a petulant two-year-old and shook his head. Slane scarcely believed the words coming out of his own mouth. Who was he to give advice to this kid? Toby probably knew more about doing the right thing than Slane had ever known. But right now, this kid focused on himself, when all around him other people had bigger problems. Slane couldn't stop his own story, bottled up for so long, from pouring out.

"Look, not everyone has a father who cares about him. Not everyone has a family watching out for them, trying to protect them, and also trying to teach them how to grow up to be a decent person." He took a deep breath and ran his fingers, dirty from digging in the mud, through his shaggy hair. He gazed toward the mountains, unable to make eye contact as he confessed, "Toby, my dad only cared that I stay out of his way or find ways to make money for him, even if they were illegal. The only thing he taught me was to fight and intimidate people into doing what he wanted them to do." He met Toby's gaze with a steely glare. "The only things he ever gave me were bruises."

The kid's face paled and his eyes widened. Yeah, this kid had led a sheltered life for all the adventure of living in this wild land.

"Be glad you have a dad who worries about you. One who's trying to teach you right from wrong. And who helps people. Don't lie to him, Toby. Don't keep things from him when he's trying to help you."

The kid nodded, but Slane doubted his lecture had made much difference. You couldn't tell a kid his age anything. At least from what he recalled, nobody could tell him anything at that age. No matter what they said, it just didn't sink in.

They continued digging, finding four more bodies before their shadows began to stretch. Toby prided himself that he hadn't barfed again, but his empty stomach had nothing left to lose.

Carlos had also carried five survivors to the clinic for treatment and now returned to pick up Slane and Joaquin. Slane gave him another stern glare before climbing into the helicopter and said, "Don't forget what I told you." Toby drew a long breath and nodded, but he wasn't about to confess and get himself in trouble.

He and Brandon jogged along behind the 4X4 as his dad let some of the older men ride back to the community. They reached the center as darkness fell.

Toby's hands felt raw, his back ached, and his stomach craved more than crackers by the time they sat down for dinner. Laila and her little brother joined them at the table, and his mother bounced the baby on her knee while trying to eat her dinner.

"How much were you able to get cleared today?" Toby's mom asked after they'd blessed the food and begun to eat.

His father took a bite and chewed quickly before answering. "Maybe a third of the way. I think it will take us at least several more days, assuming we have as many helping as we did today."

He turned to Toby. "You seemed to be having a pretty serious conversation with Joaquin's friend. What was that all about?"

Toby shrugged. "Nothing important."

His dad continued. "Carlos told me Joaquin met Slane when he joined their crew in Peru. He said Slane needed help getting away from trouble. You know Joaquin, he's always been one to look out for the underdog, take in strays, or some such thing."

"He has a tender heart. That's for sure." Toby's mom agreed.

"I hope it doesn't prove foolish. This kid seems like the kind trouble follows, if you know what I mean. He didn't seem too eager to help either," he paused, remembering Slane help him lift the man out of the mud, "but when things got tough, he stuck with it." Toby's dad usually offered praise more easily. Slane had been slow to get started, but he didn't seem to be looking for trouble. In fact, Slane kept trying to convince him to stay out of trouble. If his dad asked Slane what they talked about, Slane would probably blab about Toby's secret. Maybe it would be better if

Carlos, Joaquin, and Slane stayed home tomorrow.

Why had he shared his secret with him, anyway?

"Can I be excused?" Fear of the thoughts running through his head being revealed on his face made him eager to get away from his parents.

"Toby, you've barely eaten, and I know you must be hungry after working so hard all day." Thankfully, his father didn't mention his unfortunate barfing incident to his mom. "Please finish your meal first."

He sighed, but his growling stomach agreed, so he proceeded to stuff bites into his mouth as quickly as possible without choking. Within five minutes, with a clean plate, he asked again.

"I suppose so. You need to catch up on your studies."

"You mean, I don't even get a pass when I'm helping dig people out of a mudslide?"

Toby stifled the urge to stomp away and instead picked up his books and settled on the sofa to complete his schoolwork. Or at least to pretend to complete his schoolwork while he planned his next adventure in the village.

He thought back on his last visit before the slide. It seemed like a month had passed rather than a couple of days.

The glasman had definitely seen him peeking into the hut. What would happen if Toby returned to the village? What might the glasman do to him? His wild imagination flitted from one frightening scenario to the next. The glasmen weren't known for doing any harm. They mostly identified the cause of sickness for members of the tribe and sometimes provided herbs or rituals believed to heal. But if they blamed the illness on a person, he shuddered at the thought.

Dad had said it would take at least a few more

days to clear the road. Then they'd need to help the survivors rebuild. It would take all their efforts to complete the work in time to return to the village with Miss Maryann's next supply of medicine. Of course, Brandon would go with him, but he'd been able to ditch his big brother twice already with no problem. Next time, maybe he would tell Brandon he'd left the medicine here at the house and needed to come back and get it. Or maybe he would pretend to be sick in the village and tell Brandon he needed to come get mom and dad. He'd think of something.

He needed to go back to the spot in the woods. He wanted to get the skull he'd found. Then Slane couldn't claim it was just some dumb monkey. The guy didn't know anything, and yet he tried to tell Toby what to do? He snorted.

He also wanted to spy on the glasman again. What kind of chant had he been doing? And most importantly, was the skull he'd found connected to the glasman's chanting and smoking leaves and pig skull? Curiosity led his imagination down a path more dangerous and exciting than the trail up the mountain. He had stumbled upon a mystery, and Toby loved a mystery better than any other type of story. He'd unravel this one, no matter what.

"I heard you tell Toby to think about what you said. Said about what?" Carlos asked Slane as they walked from the helipad to the house when they returned to Kopi.

Slane shrugged. "Just trying to help him see how lucky he is."

Joaquin came alongside him. "I didn't mean to

eavesdrop, but I caught enough of it to know you've had a pretty rough time. I'm sorry."

Carlos rested his hand on Slane's shoulder. "We're here for you. Sailors have an old saying: 'If you don't know which port you're headed for, no wind is favorable.'"

"I don't understand." Slane's brow wrinkled at the riddle.

"It means you need to figure out who you are and what you want, or you will always be battling against everything but never winning."

Slane nodded as he let the words penetrate the painful memories he'd dredged up. When he considered his deepest needs, he had no idea who he was or what he wanted.

His life had been adrift, battered by winds first from his father, then the men Mara's father sent to teach him a lesson, and then Gerardo. Most recently and much less painfully, he was piloted by the captain of the MSC Katie and even by Joaquin. Both of them had been helpful and generous, but Slane was still being pushed along by someone else's plans, rather than his own. Maybe the time had come for him to determine which port to head for.

After a hot shower and a big meal, courtesy of Aunt Gloria, Slane plopped down on the leather sofa in the living room. He leaned his head back and closed his eyes.

"I have an idea." Carlos took a seat in the chair next to him, pulled the coffee table over a little closer, and placed a chess set on it. "Why don't we play a game of chess?"

Slane straightened up. "I haven't played in years.

Not sure I remember how." His mother's brother had taught him when he was nine. The memory sweetened the bitterness of his earlier reminiscences. Uncle Pietr had been good to him.

"I'm sure it will come back to you. And I'm not exactly a chess champion." Carlos chuckled and moved his first piece, a pawn.

Slane studied the board for a moment, trying to recall his uncle's lessons more than anything else. He met Carlos's pawn with his own. Carlos advanced the pawn next to his first one, and Slane captured it. Carlos slid his bishop one space beyond the reach of Slane's pawns, and Slane moved his queen onto the field of battle. Carlos moved his king to the right. Slane glanced up at him and back at the board, puzzled by Carlos's strategy. He'd left the king exposed.

Slane advanced a pawn, and instantly regretted it as Carlos took it with his bishop. Slane took a deep breath and moved his knight. The older man mirrored his move. Slane slid his queen deeper into enemy territory, looking up to watch Carlos for any reaction.

Slane managed to capture both of Carlos's rooks and one bishop. Carlos moved his remaining pieces, closing in on Slane's king.

Slane grinned when Carlos moved his queen into a spot within reach of Slane's knight. He'd barely scooped up the queen when Carlos slid his remaining bishop into place, blocking his king's only exit. Slane slapped his knee and bit his tongue to keep from saying the word which came to mind.

"I can't believe you sacrificed your queen!"

Carlos laughed. "It's an old, but effective strategy. When the stakes are high, we reveal what we are willing to surrender. And what is most important to us."

Slane nodded as he pondered the words. "I'm not sure what you mean."

"When I was a young man, like you, I loved being onboard the ship, visiting different ports, and seeing the world. When I met my wife, I realized that in order to have a life with her, I had to give up my life on the sea."

He paused, as if remembering another time and place. "When my brother and his wife died, and Joaquin was left homeless, I had to make sacrifices in order to find him, bring him here, and provide for him. I had to decide what mattered most in those moments: my desires or someone I love?"

He smiled. "God faced the same decision. When mankind sinned, it separated us from God. He chose to sacrifice His own Son in order to bridge the divide because He loved us.

"When the stakes were high, God revealed what He was willing to sacrifice," he repeated.

Slane frowned. A God who loved people and chose them over His own Son? It didn't make sense. "That sounds crazy. Why would God do that? He's God. He can do whatever He wants, right?"

Carlos nodded. "That's what is so amazing. God can do whatever He wants, and what He wants is to have a relationship with you and me. It does sound crazy, because you and I know we don't deserve such amazing love. We know in our hearts and minds, and even in our actions, we've broken God's laws, disrespected God, and even rebelled against Him and rejected Him."

Slane couldn't argue with that. He knew with crystal clarity the terrible things he had done. Darkness lingered in his soul.

"So, if we don't deserve his love, why would he punish his son for our mistakes?"

"The Bible says it's because God so loved the world in John 3:16." Carlos reached for the drawer in the coffee table and pulled out a Bible. Slane stiffened. He appreciated everything Carlos, Gloria, and Joaquin had done for him, but he didn't need them to start quoting the Bible to him.

He yawned, trying to make it appear natural rather than forced. He'd worked hard today, after all. "Thanks, Carlos, but I'm going to get some sleep. Good night." He hurried up the stairs before Carlos had time to respond. As he climbed in the bed, though, the conversation reverberated in his mind like an echo through a canyon, dislodging his pride and bringing a landslide of emotions.

CHAPTER NINE

Toby continued to dig alongside his father. Three days into their work, they shifted from the portion of the slide where Haedi once stood to the road itself. Without the road, the medicines they depended on at the clinic must be delivered by helicopter, an expensive proposition, and they'd barely cleared half of the road. With each passing day, fewer villagers joined the crew and more rocks fell down to block what they had dug out the day before. Slane and Joaquin returned to help, but Toby tried to keep his distance. He didn't need any more of the newcomer's advice.

"Where is Iatmul? And Samson and Elsen?" A whine crept into his voice as Toby glanced over the group and counted more than half were from the institute.

His father glanced around and shrugged. "They may be working at the village. You know there is more than enough work to go 'round. We need some of them to help with the injured at the clinic, and others are trying to rebuild their own homes. That is their priority now. The road is most critical to us, but not most urgent to those in Haedi."

Toby grumbled some more but kept digging.

The sun had reached its peak and left a trail of sweat down his back when he looked up to see Samson running toward them from the village.

"Come, we need your help. We have found someone alive! Come quickly. We need all the hands we can get," Samson shouted.

They grabbed their shovels and followed him

back down the slope, running and sliding in the muddy grass. When they stopped, Toby couldn't believe his eyes.

The huts had been washed away by the mudslide, but as it destroyed them, the remnants of each one piled into the next and formed a dam. Eventually, the flow had overwhelmed that as well. A pile of debris the size of a large room resulted, sealed with a thick layer of mud over it.

As Samson and Elsen had scooped away mud, the debris shifted, crashing down onto a man trapped inside the tomb. The man's hoarse cries for help reached them as they drew near.

"He says the collapse has pinned his legs, but his upper body is still free, and he can breathe. If we cause it to collapse more, he will be buried alive."

Samson pointed at Toby. "You, come here and hold these branches up." Toby obeyed, stepping into the mud and sinking to his shins. Samson directed Slane next, setting him opposite Toby and asking him to hold the far end of the same section of what had once been the wall of a home. One by one, he stationed the volunteers in the midst of the flow to support the weight of the debris and keep it from collapsing. Next, he and several others began digging to free the survivor, whose screams grew weaker by the minute.

It took an hour to reach the man, and Toby's arms grew weary of the weight.

"I see him!" Samson called from the hole he had dug. "I'm going to try to move the branches on his legs and get him free." The cries stopped, and Toby hoped the man had stopped yelling because he saw the rescue so close at hand.

As Samson dug, Toby shifted his weight and a cascade of mud and debris sifted down on the two men. Samson called out, "Don't move! If this shifts, we will be buried!" Toby locked his arms and kept as still as possible.

As Samson removed the branches and mud from the man's legs, the pile shifted again, tilting precariously at an angle. For a moment, which seemed to last forever, no sound of movement came from under the debris. Then he heard a rustling in the pile, and Samson burst through the hole he had dug, dragging the man behind him.

As soon as they cleared the flow, Toby's strength gave way, and the branches slipped from his grasp. The structure shifted, and the other men lost their grips as well until the whole monstrosity of debris came crashing down inches from where Samson and the survivor had collapsed.

Toby and the others slogged out of the mire as the mud oozed into the void.

Toby's dad knelt by the man who had been rescued. He lay deathly still; he didn't even seem to be breathing. Toby's dad listened to the man's chest. "He's alive." He pulled his shirt off and used it to wipe the mud off the man's face and away from his mouth and nostrils. Listening again for a breath, he shook his head and hollered, "Get something we can carry him on. Carlos, we're going to need to transport him to the clinic." People sprang into action around him as Toby watched his father begin blowing air into the man's lungs.

Samson and Elsen disappeared and returned with a flat piece of wood, long enough to bear most of the man. His dad paused in his rescue breathing and listened again. "I think he's breathing on his own, but it's weak." The man's parched lips and sunken eyes testified to the days he'd gone without water. Toby's dad held his head and eased the water bottle to his cracked lips, then took off his own shirt and soaked the one clean sleeve with water from his water bottle. He wiped the mud from the man's face with the moist cloth.

They heaved the man gently onto the piece of wood and carried it to the chopper. The four men reminded Toby of the pallbearers at a funeral, each of them holding an edge of the makeshift gurney.

Toby's dad hopped into the chopper beside the man to continue to monitor him until they reached the clinic. As the copter took off, the grass swirled around them like a dirt devil, and Toby shielded his eyes. It had been three whole days since the landslide, and somehow the man had survived.

What if others were trapped? His frustration over all the hard work of digging the mud and rocks out faded away. They had helped save a man's life!

He clapped his hands together and turned to Brandon, Slane, and Joaquin who stood watching the helicopter. "I guess we need to get back to work." He didn't wait to hear their response but turned and headed back to where they had left their shovels.

By evening, they had cleared most of the debris away from the roadbed. The asphalt itself had been ripped away, carried somewhere farther down the valley, so their work would also include leveling the path through the debris and eventually getting new asphalt spread, but it might be months before they could get the materials to resurface the road.

They hiked back to the institute, checking in at the clinic to learn their survivor had been airlifted to Mount Hagen. Carlos would be back to get Joaquin and Slane after he delivered the man to the hospital.

Toby's dad invited them to dinner, and Toby gave

his full attention to the conversation, still nervous about his secret being revealed.

"Thanks for the invitation, but I hate to impose again." Joaquin shifted uncomfortably, and Toby remembered Amy's strange behavior when they'd had dinner night before last.

"Nonsense! It's the least we can do after you've worked so hard to help us clear the road," Dad insisted.

"The road is essential for all of us. Without it, Uncle Carlos won't be able to transport the coffee once it is ready for processing. The green coffee is almost ready for transport to Port Moresby. If we cannot deliver it in time, the whole crop might be lost." Joaquin continued, "We can't even get back to Kopi except by chopper until the road is fixed."

"I hadn't even thought of that. How has the harvest been this year? We've had so much rain." Toby's father opened the door of the clinic.

They filed out the door and started up the road toward Toby's house as Joaquin answered. "Uncle Carlos mentioned it had been really wet this year, but it's been a good harvest. I'm more concerned the seeds won't dry before they begin to go bad. Between the rains and now some of our workers having to rebuild, they aren't drying as quickly as they usually do. But I know Uncle Carlos is trusting the Lord. I guess that is all we can do sometimes."

"Once we get the road cleared, maybe we can return the favor by helping your employees rebuild their homes and then pitching in with them to get your coffee ready for shipment."

"That would be a great help."

Great. Now his dad had volunteered them not only to help with the road and the village, but to help

Carlos with his coffee as well. Toby crossed his arms and let out a sigh loud enough to draw a frown from his dad. He sped up his pace to get ahead of the others and avoid a confrontation, but Slane caught up to him.

"So, have you told your father about the bone you found?" Slane whispered, but Toby still glanced over his shoulder to be sure his father wasn't listening. Dad appeared to be deep in conversation with Joaquin about coffee or something equally boring. Toby pressed his lips together and shook his head before answering.

"Not yet."

"Toby, you don't know how lucky you are to have such a great family. Especially your dad. He cares about you."

Toby caught the tinge of longing and wondered about the pain Slane had hinted at. He shook his head. "He cares about other people, and volunteering me to help them."

Slane snorted and shot back. "Or maybe he's trying to teach you something about helping people and being a man. Besides, what is so bad about caring about other people? The world needs a little more of that."

The sound of Carlos arriving in the helicopter cut the conversation short, and Toby smiled as Joaquin and Slane turned around and headed back toward the field near the clinic.

"We'll have to take a raincheck on dinner, but thanks for the offer." Joaquin waved, but Slane locked eyes with Toby and then cut his gaze toward Toby's dad. Toby ignored him and hurried home.

Amy watched her father and brothers walking toward the house with Joaquin and Slane as she scrubbed the skins of the kaukau. She tried to ignore the pinch of disappointment when she heard the thwak-thwak-thwak of the helicopter and saw a certain tall, lanky figure turn back.

Why can't I just ignore him? It's just curiosity, nothing more! Slane's face kept popping into her mind at the oddest moments. The strange familiarity of his name teased her like a memory hid just beyond her reach. *Argh! It was driving her nuts.*

She shook her head at her own silliness and returned to the work of preparing dinner for the family while her mother continued to help at the clinic. By the time the men had cleaned the mud and grime from their hands and faces and changed clothes, Amy had dinner ready.

Laila carried a basket of the food from dinner to share with her mother at the clinic, taking her brother and sister along. She and her siblings had settled in, the two girls sharing a sleeping bag on the floor in Amy's room. Amy had offered to give up her bed, but Laila had said she couldn't sleep on the soft mattress. It reminded Amy of how soft a life she lived compared to her friends.

The absence of her mother's cheerful voice created a quiet and somber mood at the table. The physical and emotional toll of the day had left them all exhausted.

Her father broke the silence. "This is good, Amy. You've outdone yourself."

"Thank you." She smiled. They ate the same meal

most nights, but she appreciated the compliment and the opportunity to think about something else. "I made too much. I thought we'd have company."

"I invited Joaquin and his buddy, but Carlos returned from his run to Mount Hagen in time to pick them up. They've been a huge help on the road. Not sure we could do it without them." Amy noticed how his assessment of the troublemaker improved each day.

She shivered at the recollection of the mud flowing down over the village, a wall of destruction. Would the villagers be able to start over after so much destruction? She wasn't sure what she could do, but she wanted to help her friend.

"Have they started to rebuild the village? I know Laila and Moia will need help. I guess it will be safe for them to stay in Haedi since Nizax is gone."

Her father paused with the fork loaded with kaukau mid-air. "Nizax? I think he's the one we pulled out of the rubble today. It was a miracle he survived so long, but I think he'll be fine. What does he have to do with Laila?"

Amy swallowed the lump in her throat. Her mind raced ahead toward recovery and building a new life. But for the villagers, the focus remained on futile attempts to rescue their loved ones, or simply to bury the dead. Now Nizax posed a threat to her friend's family. She relayed her conversation with Laila in the moments before the landslide to her father. "Dad, if he makes Laila go back to Wara and marry him, what will happen to her?"

"He regained consciousness by the time we got to the outpost. He kept praising God for saving him, saying he had seen Jesus when he was buried under the slide. Carlos took him to Mount Hagen because he was so dehydrated, and our little clinic is full. I sent word to your mom to notify his family, but she said no one knew the name. I guess it's no surprise Moia didn't admit she knew him. He'll be in Mount Hagen for a day or two recovering."

Amy's stomach felt full and queasy, and she pushed the plate away. "But he's alive. He can go back to Wara and tell them where Moia is."

Her father nodded grimly. "We need to pray for him. God is up to something with that young man. We'll have to find out what he plans to do and whether it endangers Moia and her family."

"May I be excused?" She mumbled even as she cleared her dishes from the table.

"Sure. I'm sorry, honey." Her father's guilty expression prompted her to give him a quick hug.

"It's fine. Really. I'm just worried for Laila. She's lost so much already." The lump in her throat kept her from saying any more.

After piling her dishes on the counter, she sat down at the computer.

Escaping her island home, even if only online, seemed to be the best way to take her mind off Nizax and the danger to Laila. She clicked away on the computer until she landed on the International Mission Force website. Reading through the prayer requests and praises of friends she had never met put her own situation in perspective. She scanned through their stories of political upheaval, threats from terrorists, and efforts to thwart human trafficking. She posted a quick update, telling of her narrow escape from the landslide and asking for prayer for the village and her friend's family in particular.

Typing the words brought courage and strength to keep going. Soon, comments popped up, including words of encouragement and prayers for her and Laila. She felt the prayers of brothers and sisters around the globe rising to heaven and carrying her worries and cares with them.

By the time her allotted time on the laptop expired, peace enveloped her like a warm blanket on a cold night.

CHAPTER TEN

Toby stared at the ceiling, his fingers turning the tiny bone over and over as he thought about his conversation with Slane. A part of him recognized the truth, but he shoved the harsh reality away.

It didn't fit with his plans. Telling his father what he'd been up to would certainly end his adventure and likely land him in deep trouble with his dad.

Besides, he could handle this. He didn't need help, and he didn't need advice from some guy who thought he had Toby all figured out.

Instead, he needed a plan for getting back to the village to spy on the glasman again. But his father had committed him to work on the road, and then the village, and then help at Carlos' coffee plantation. Resentment settled in his gut like a tight knot, and bile rose in his throat.

His imagination flitted back to the image of the glasman sitting by his fire, waving the smoking weeds and chanting. What if he really did have the power to see what caused people to be ill? Was it magic? Was there any truth to the miracle he'd seen when the glasman seemed to cure the man?

Toby had seen the sick villager tell the glasman where he had pain, and after smoking and shaking and going into a trance, the glasman snatched the pain out. He showed the sick man a stone he said he had pulled out of him, and the man seemed to be healed.

Even though Toby knew it was crazy to believe in such magic, his own eyes had witnessed it. The sense of something magical and mystical in the old man's work clung to his imagination, and his desire to solve the mystery grew.

"Brandon," he whispered to see if his brother was awake. Hearing no response, he slipped silently from under the covers and out the door. Maybe he could find out more by searching online.

The moon cast bluish light through the windows, and Toby knew every step in the small house, allowing him to reach the computer without turning on lights or stepping on any of the creaky floorboards. He touched the power button and winced at the slight whirring sound roaring to life in the stillness of the night. The digital clock on the screen read just past midnight, and everyone was sound asleep.

A few quick clicks on the keyboard and he found an article about glasmen. The site portrayed missionaries like his family as destroying the traditional way of life through their spread of the gospel. Instead, this website claimed to celebrate the nobility of traditional cultures, but it didn't mention the violence and self-destruction. It didn't mention the women he'd heard his parents whisper about who had been tortured and killed because a glasman identified them as witches.

He shivered despite the warmth of the house.

The article praised those who resisted the influence of Westerners and maintained their centuries-old traditions. It referenced the glasman's claims to travel outside his body in his dreams and commune with spirits as proven facts.

Toby pondered the idea. He'd had dreams similar to what they described, where it felt like he zoomed through the air, guiding his flight just by willing himself in one direction or another. It was amazing. He imagined it felt similar to hang-gliding on the colorful kites they had seen in Queensland when they visited Australia a few years back.

But unlike when he had watched the hang gliders, he'd had no fear in the dream. He saw the village far below him. He soared far above the tallest trees; yet peace carried him along like he was floating on a cloud. Imagine being able to do that anytime you wanted! Fascination, bordering on obsession, drew him into the story.

Toby read more, scouring the internet for stories about the glasman, about sanguma, and other traditional New Guinean rituals. The more he read, the faster his heart raced as fear and mystery and curiosity converged to send adrenalin pumping through his veins. His palms became moist, and he dried them on his pajama pants. He closed his eyes and rubbed them to ease the burning sensation. Staring at the glow of the screen in a dark room was a bad idea, especially when he had left his glasses in his room.

A yawn stretched his mouth wide, and when he snapped it shut and opened his eyes, his father stood in the doorway, arms folded across his chest.

"What are you doing on the computer at this time of night?"

Toby's father's voice had a groggy but still angry quality which confirmed he'd been awakened from a sound sleep.

Toby clicked the x to close the screens he'd been viewing. "I . . .I couldn't sleep, and I thought I would check online and try to finish my research for the school paper I'm writing. You know, during the day, I'm always competing with Brandon and Amy for time on the computer." He shut down the power and yawned again, though he sensed his father's skepticism. "But I'm feeling tired now. I think I'll go back to bed."

His father's eyes narrowed, studying Toby intently like a tough puzzle he needed to solve. He held Toby's gaze for a long moment. Finally, he spoke; each word measured carefully.

"Toby, is there anything else you need to tell me? You know how I feel about you hiding things from me. If you clicked on websites you know better than to visit—"

Toby interrupted him. "Dad! Really?" His face flushed at his dad's assumption. "I was doing research for school." He let out a disgusted grunt and tried to move past his father, but his dad stepped into his path.

"Okay. So, what is your paper about, Son?" His voice didn't sound angry anymore, just very quiet, like he hoped for an answer to ease his worries.

Toby crossed his arms, mirroring his father's stance. "It's about traditional Papua New Guinea medicine. I was researching information on the glasmen and glasmeri."

His father's face softened in relief, and Toby felt a twinge of guilt as his dad drew him into a hug goodnight. He'd spoken the truth. He did have to write a paper for his history class. And now he knew what the topic would be. So he hadn't lied exactly, had he?

Amy hurried down the hill toward the village to find Laila. Samson had offered to help rebuild Moia's home so she would have a place to recuperate from her injuries. Laila and her brother had left baby Isa with Moia at the clinic and set out for the village before the sun rose. She found them collecting pieces of wood to rebuild their home and stacking them near an areca tree.

Amy joined her friend, scavenging for any materials they might find useful. The field at the edge of the mudslide provided a pile of wood where those who searched for survivors had tossed the debris along the bank. Amy gathered all the pieces on the bank and piled them near the spot they cleared for the hut.

She went back to the mudflow and searched for more usable pieces. Pulling a few branches out of the mud near the edge, she tossed them on the bank, then slipped off her shoes and stepped carefully onto a rock at the edge of the debris field to reach for a branch protruding from the soupy mess. Tugging gently, then harder, she pulled it loose and tossed it back toward the grass.

She found several other branches she could reach before she had to find another rock and step further into the field to retrieve more. Soon her pile of wood near the edge of the mud grew, and she perched on a rock in the middle of the mudflow.

As she reached for another limb, she caught sight of a tall, reed-thin figure topping the hill. Joaquin walked beside him.

Should she wave? Call out hello?

Her hands felt suddenly sweaty, and she brushed a strand of hair from her face without thinking about the thick gray mud she left behind. She tried to wipe the mud off with the back of her hand, but it only made it worse.

What did she care, anyway? She should be helping her friend rebuild her home, not obsessing about a guy who'd be gone in another week.

She rolled her eyes, frustrated with her own

distraction, and returned to her task. A log, the trunk of a tree wiped out by the landslide, seemed to be the next opportunity for a foothold. It lay about a yard from the rock she perched on, and she reached her bare toes as far as possible to grasp the rough surface of the log. With a grunt, she sprang off her current base, trying not to think about the graceless picture she presented.

At the last second, the rock she'd been standing on sank into the muck and threw her off balance. Instead of landing on the log she had aimed for, she landed with one leg stuck up to her knee and the other resting atop the mud. When she tried to shift her weight to her free foot and stand up, her foot sank straight down, taking her even deeper into the mud.

Her predicament went from a silly mishap to a terrifying nightmare in a flash. The more she tried to pull her legs out of the slime, the deeper she sank. Panic set in. Her heart raced, and her breath caught. Thigh-deep in the debris, the wet slime sucked at her legs like a monster trying to swallow her whole.

She scanned the area but didn't see Samson or Laila's brother anywhere. In the distance, Joaquin shouted to be still as he and Slane ran toward her. She tried to inhale deeply and control the fear crushing her chest, as deadly as the mud. She turned back toward the hill and fixed her gaze on the two figures racing toward her. They were too far away. Her hips sank into the mire, and she concentrated on being still. Only her lips moved as she prayed desperately for God to keep her feet from sinking further.

The image of Laila's mother curled up in the mud came to mind, but if she tried to curl up, would she sink more?

Calm. Calm. Calm.

Pray. Pray. Pray.

But no words would come except, "Help." So, she prayed over and over. "Help me, Lord. Please help me."

Laila must have heard Joaquin's screams because she ran from the forest and raced to rescue her friend. Nimbly hopping from one rock to the next until she reached Amy, she held out her hand and Amy grabbed it and held on. Laila began to pull, and for a brief second, Amy felt the mud loosen its grip a tiny bit.

But Laila was much smaller than Amy and lacked the strength to pull her out. The ooze sucked Amy even deeper, pulling Laila off balance. Amy tried to help steady her, but her friend landed right beside her, the sludge greedily sucking her in as well.

Now both of them stood waist deep. Laila flailed about just as Amy had, trying to get out and sinking them both further.

Amy grabbed both sides of her friend's face and caught her eyes. "Stop moving." Her words sounded so much like her father's calm, strong presence she thought for a moment he was with her. "We have to be as still as we can." Laila nodded and tears tracked down her face through the mud. Amy brushed them away with her own muddy hand. "We're going to be okay."

She didn't know why she said it. She didn't believe it for a minute, but the panic in Laila's eyes tore at her heart. If they were going to die like this, sinking in this stinking mud, at least they would not hasten it with their fear. Her thoughts belied her calm exterior as the faces of those she loved came to mind.

Her parents.

Her sister and brothers.

Her friends.

Her frantic thoughts finally rested on the Lord. If she died here today, she would be with the Lord. Peace engulfed her as it had the night before when she'd asked her friends online to pray for her.

But Laila.

Amy's heart lurched.

They were chest-deep now.

And Laila didn't know the Lord. Amy had focused on developing their friendship. She had taken it slowly, thinking she had plenty of time. Laila had come to church with her and enjoyed learning about Jesus. She'd been eager and so interested in what Amy believed and why she believed it, but Amy had never asked her if she believed it too. Why had she never asked her? What if time ran out?

She took a deep breath and began. "Laila, I know you've come to church with me and my family and you've asked me about what I believe—"

Her friend interrupted. "I have heard the pastor when he asks if anyone wants to follow Jesus. I want to do that! If I die today, I want to be with Jesus!"

"Do you believe Jesus has done everything needed for you to be saved?" Amy held her friend's hands tight as the mud squished up under their arms.

Her friend nodded.

"And are you willing to go wherever He leads you to go and do whatever He leads you to do?" The words she'd heard her father repeat when he baptized her resonated profoundly in this moment. Laila glanced around them and said in a strong voice, "Yes." Her journey would resemble the thief on the cross next to Jesus more than an evangelist.

"You are now my sister in Christ."

Amy wanted to hug her friend, to jump up and

down, but the sludge kept on sucking. She'd lost sight of Joaquin and Slane and didn't dare turn to look. Still holding Laila's hands, she raised them above their heads and waited for the mud to reach her chin. She closed her eyes and began to pray again, whispering words only she and the Lord comprehended.

A warm hand covered both her hand and Laila's. Amy turned her head, afraid to move anything else. Slane and Joaquin had used the pile of wood she had collected to fashion a makeshift pier from the edge of the mud to the midst of the debris. Slane lay on his belly to distribute his weight. His head and arm reached beyond the last board to grasp their hands. Joaquin scuttled back and forth on his hands and knees, handing Slane wood as needed to move closer to the trapped girls.

Slane pulled their hands toward him, dragging them through the mud.

"Try to stretch out flat near the surface, if you can," Joaquin called to them.

"I can only pull one of you out at a time." Slane met Amy's gaze as she pushed her friend toward him.

"She's lighter. It will be easier to pull her out first." Slane tucked his chin and pulled Laila until her head and shoulders rested on the plank beside him. She wiggled and squirmed her way onto the plank and then crawled until she reached safety.

All her movement churned up the mud, and Amy slipped deeper into the mire. She lifted her chin as high as she could and pressed her lips together as the slime threatened to drown her.

"Okay. Your turn."

Amy reached for Slane's hand, but the void Laila left had sucked her farther away. Her fingers brushed the ends of his, and the mud masked her sealed lips.

She arched her neck to keep her nose free and sucked in air as she reached for him again. No matter how hard she stretched, he was out of reach.

Slane scooted closer and reached again, their fingertips barely making contact as the mud covered her ears. Tears blinded her, and her arms flailed, searching for her rescuer. A fabric sleeve swatted her face.

"Grab hold!" Slane shouted as he held the other sleeve of the shirt he had shed. She gripped the cuff and held perfectly still, afraid any movement would suck her back down, as he pulled her out of the mud onto the wooden lifeline.

With her arms and chest on the planks, she let go of the shirt and army crawled until her whole body rested atop the plank beside him.

Her legs trembled, and every muscle ceased to function at her command. Her entire body rebelled against her brain. She tried to push herself up onto her hands and knees, but they wouldn't hold. Her knees buckled, and she slumped on the rough wood. The panic, fighting the mud, and maybe the trauma itself had left her temporarily paralyzed. The wood on which she rested settled deeper in the mud and panic crept in again.

"I can't move."

Slane scuttled backward down the length of wood alongside her until his shoulders neared hers. He raised up on his knees and reached over her to grasp the edges of the piece she lay on. His shoulders hovered over her and blocked out the sun but not its warmth. The snake tattoo which had fascinated Ruth stared back at her.

Lifting the end of her board onto the next piece and backing up on hands and knees, he pulled her along as she clung to the wood. He continued inching back, the tendons in his arms flexing on either side of her as he dragged the board. It sank under her weight, and she let out a whimper as the mud tugged at her feet, but each inch brought her closer to safety. It seemed like forever, and she felt guilty for not contributing at all, but any movement would send her back into the sludge.

They neared the edge of the mudslide, and Slane rose and took her hand. He pulled her to her feet, but her legs buckled like a newborn fawn. Slipping an arm around her before she could protest, he scooped her muddy form into his arms. She wrapped her arm around his neck to hang on. Her fingers brushed the raised, smooth skin of a scar across his shoulders, and she jerked her hand away. Her blue eyes searched his dark ones but found no answers, just a hidden pain as if the wound was fresh.

He carried her to where Laila sat on the grass, scraping the mud veneer from her body with a small stick. Slane lowered Amy to the ground carefully, like he feared she might shatter. The sudden absence of his warm arms and the cool of the mud made her shudder. He turned away and slipped his shirt back on, but not before she caught a glimpse of the marks crisscrossing his back.

Amy grabbed her friend in a muddy embrace and tried not to think of how he'd gotten such scars. She tried to wipe some of the mud off Laila's face and giggled as her effort only added a layer. Laila stared at her like she'd lost her mind. As Amy surveyed their mud-covered clothes and reflected on how close they'd come to being buried alive, her emotions spiraled out of control. Relief flooded over her with an intensity that took her breath away.

Laila voiced the joy and freedom they both felt. "We're alive! We're alive. And now we are sisters in Christ."

Overwhelmed by so much more than just surviving, joy, pain, relief, gratitude, fear, and exhaustion swirled into a cyclone which left Amy hysterical over the miracle of their rescue. Her giggles bubbled into uncontrolled laughter and then spiraled into tears. Not just quiet sobs either. The maelstrom of emotions overcame her, and she blubbered like a toddler. She lay on the grass and let the torrent carry her away.

Joaquin and Slane stood several paces away, pulling the planks of wood back out of the mud and piling them again on the grass. They turned as the sound of her sobs caught their attention. Just when Amy started to regain control, she saw their concerned frowns. Her face flushed, and she wiped at the tears with her muddy hands, trying to get it together.

Joaquin squatted beside her and waited for her to calm down. When she finally stilled after a few final giggles, he used the tail of his shirt to wipe the dirt from her face.

"You okay now?" He made eye contact and when she nodded, he helped her to her feet. Her legs trembled but held steady.

"No more trying to fetch anything you can't reach from the edge." His somber tone felt like her father scolding her. "Are we clear?"

She resisted the stubborn urge to balk at his admonition. He was right. She nodded and hugged him tightly.

"Thank you." Her eyes cut over to Slane as she let go. "Thank you both."

Slane acknowledged her gratitude with a dip of his head and looked away like she had embarrassed him.

They retrieved the rest of the wood and piled it up for rebuilding while Amy and Laila scraped the drying mud from their skin and clothes.

Slane and Joaquin must have decided she hadn't lost her mind after all, because they returned to searching for materials to use in the rebuilding effort. Amy watched as Slane hauled a large branch over to the pile, the muscles in his arms popping as they had when he pulled her to safety. The memory of being swooped up and rescued by those strong arms stuck with her as she and Laila resumed their work.

CHAPTER ELEVEN

Slane paused after hauling a large branch back to the pile and ran his muddy hand through his hair. He instantly regretted it. He tried wiping the muck from his hand onto his shorts, but it didn't help. Mud smeared his shirt and shorts from lifting Amy out of the mire. He shook his head.

Did she realize how close she and Laila came to dying? If he and Joaquin had been five minutes later, it would have been too late.

Samson and Rayz returned with an armload of wood and a long coil of dried vine, and Samson nodded at the pile of wood they'd accumulated. Apparently oblivious to Amy and Laila's brush with catastrophe, he squatted and began joining pieces of wood together with the vine. He called Laila over to help Rayz hold the pieces as he joined them together and frowned as he took in her mud-bathed clothes.

She must have explained what happened because he stared up at Slane with a betel-nut-stained smile and nodded with gratitude.

Slane and Joaquin watched Samson line up a piece of wood, wrap the vine from the previous piece around the next, and tie it off. Joaquin called Amy to help hold them as Laila did. Samson worked quickly and completed a section while Slane, Joaquin, and Amy tried to figure out how to tie the vine tight enough to hold the wood in place without snapping the vine in two.

It took three of them to accomplish what Samson did in half the time, but they finally got the hang of it and completed a section of wall. Samson motioned for them to follow and hefted his section over his head as he led them to a higher elevation where several other families were rebuilding as well.

Slane admired the organization of their efforts. They had chosen an open field, reasonably level, with trees and the river nearby. They left space at one end and built their huts, facing one another in an arc, creating a sort of "main street" leading to the open space which would serve for community gatherings.

Joaquin pointed to the field. "Before the missionaries came, the field would include a spirit house where worship would take place, but most of this tribe has come to faith. They will rebuild a place to worship as soon as their homes are completed." Slane didn't comment on their priorities.

He followed Samson and copied his efforts as he used a large rock to pound a long, straight piece of wood into the ground. They paced off several feet and drove another support into the ground. The process continued until a dozen poles stood in a large circle. The man used the woody vine to lash the section he had built to the first pole and then to the next closest one. He showed Joaquin and Slane how to hold one section of the wall up while they used more vines to join it with the next section. As the sun began to sink over the mountains, they had what amounted to a ring of walls with no roof.

Slane had focused so intently on the work that he startled when Joaquin nudged him and pointed toward the shades of orange in the west, fading to deep blue with a single star peeking out in the east. His friend called out to Amy, "We need to hurry if we are going to get you and Laila home before the gate closes." She glanced down at her mud-caked clothes and wrinkled her nose in a way which shouldn't have been so attractive. He thought of her parents asking for an explanation and smiled at the thought of her telling her father about his role in the story. Imagine him playing the hero. There was a first time for everything.

Amy awoke to the sun streaming through her window and her body aching. Whether from the ordeal or the labor of building a home, she wasn't sure. Her stomach rumbled, reminding her how little she'd eaten despite working so hard.

Breakfast waited on the table—sago pancakes and bananas. Her father and brothers had already eaten and left for the road detail as soon as the sun came up. Her mother stood at the sink, rinsing her plate.

"Good morning. I thought I might miss you. I'm headed to the clinic. Laila's mom is able to put weight on her leg and doesn't want to go to Mount Hagen for an x-ray. And she definitely does not want to go back up in the helicopter again." She chuckled. "I think her leg is healing well, and she will be released today."

"Oh, that's great. We may be able to finish rebuilding their home today. We got the walls up yesterday."

"Wonderful. I'm sure she will be glad to see what you've done." Her mother's voice sounded flat, worn down by the long days and the injuries she'd witnessed but couldn't heal. Amy winced when she hugged her, and her mother paused. "Are you okay?"

"Sure. I'm just not used to all this hard work." Amy tried to brush it off. She hadn't wanted to worry them about her brush with danger, so she'd explained away the mud-covered clothing last night with a fib about slipping in the mud. Technically, she had slipped in the mud. She just omitted the details about how close she came to being buried in it.

Her foolishness in having gone out on the mudflow to begin with brought a flush of warmth to her cheeks. Her mother gave her the side-eye, a sure sign of her doubts about Amy's excuse. The demands of the clinic must have weighed heavy on her, though, because she hurried out the door without pursuing it further.

After breakfast, Amy packed a box of bush biscuits and started the trek back to the village with Laila and her brother. Her muscles protested every step of the way, but nothing deterred her from helping her friend rebuild Moia's home. Finally, her work meant something. Though her body ached, her heart overflowed with satisfaction.

She thought back on Laila's profession of faith. It had been such a moment of panic, but was her friend's salvation for real?

"Laila, remember what happened when we were sinking in the mud? I know we were both scared, but I don't want you to feel like I pressured you into saying a prayer if you didn't mean it."

Her friend smiled up at her. "I meant it with all my heart. In fact, I spoke to the pastor while he visited Mami last night. I am going to be baptized this Sunday after services. I told Mami what had happened and how God rescued us, and she has placed her faith in God as well."

Amy marveled at how a single event impacted both Laila's and her mother's lives for eternity. But as they neared the site where the community had begun rebuilding, fear crept in. They would complete the home for Moia, but would Laila be able to live in Haedi with her mother, and her brother and sister? Or would Nizax come and take her back to Wara as his child-bride? She had to warn Laila that Nizax survived.

"Laila, Dad said they pulled Nizax out of the rubble, and he is going to be fine. Carlos took him to Mount Hagen, but he will be released soon."

"Yes. Mami said she heard he had survived. Now she thinks maybe I should marry him since we have lost everything. Otherwise, how will we survive?" Laila's calm voice hid her panic, but her eyes darted toward the mountain, toward Wara, and the life awaiting her.

Amy wanted to tell Laila to trust in the Lord, but she knew trusting God didn't mean things always worked out the way you want. She wanted to encourage her to refuse the arranged marriage, but she knew Moia's fears were real. She wanted to promise her friend she could fix all these problems, but instead she said, "I'm sorry," and walked alongside her in silence.

Samson had made significant progress by the time they arrived. He used the liana to tie lengths of wood together at a central point, which would be the center of their roof, while Laila and Amy scavenged through the sparse trees and the mudflow for additional pieces to complete the circle.

Amy returned to the building site with an armload of wood. Slane and Joaquin helped Samson raise the roof and use the liana to anchor it to the walls they had assembled the day before. Once they secured the frame all the way around the circular structure, they would add the thatch to the roof, layering kunai grass over the spokes of the wooden frame.

Amy, Laila, and Rayz harvested the kunai grass from the seemingly endless supply in the fields nearby. As they brought each armful of the grass back to the house, Joaquin and Slane used blades of the grass to tie wads of grass together in a bunch. Then they handed the bunch to Samson, who had climbed the structure and squatted on the frame, where he received and tied each bundle to the frame. Amy marveled at the structure holding his weight. It never wavered as he moved. The lightweight, tough grass provided a thick roof, and Samson worked quickly from the lowest circle overhanging the walls toward the peak.

As the sun grew warm, Laila ventured off to check on her garden. The villagers shared a community garden which had been spared the destruction of the mudslide because of its location higher up the mountain opposite the landslide and to the east of the village. She returned with several kaukau to share with them.

Samson climbed down, and they squatted in the shade of the hut and nibbled on the snack Amy had brought. Smoke drifted through the unfinished roof as Laila lit a small fire in the center of the hut and roasted some kaukau from her garden to complete their meal.

Slane accepted the crunchy bush biscuit Amy offered and the welcomed rest from their hard work all morning. Despite not getting to enjoy a leisurely shore leave resting up for his rigorous job onboard the Katie, his initial ambivalence about all the labor Joaquin and Carlos had planned for him had vanished. He'd discovered that work, which included saving someone from certain death or providing a home for a family who'd lost everything, came with its own rewards.

One of those rewards came in the form of the smile Amy shared along with the biscuit.

"I'm surprised your parents didn't insist you stay at the institute after yesterday." He flipped the lock of hair out of his face and watched her reaction. But she avoided his gaze and her cheeks turned pink enough to be visible even in the dim light of the hut.

"I told them I slipped in the mud. I didn't want them to worry about it. They have enough to deal with right now with treating those who are hurt at the clinic and rebuilding the road."

He nodded. It made sense, even sounded unselfish to be so concerned with her parents' worries, and he certainly couldn't pass judgment on her pretense. He'd bent the truth plenty of times.

So why did he feel as though he had been sucker-punched in the gut? His one act of heroism had been stolen. Erased.

A voice whispered to his soul that no good deed is rewarded. He should care for his own needs, not the hardships of others. The satisfaction of helping others evaporated under the heat of his anger.

He caught Joaquin staring at him and needed to escape his friend's scrutiny. Murmuring an excuse, he uncoiled his legs and rose to leave the hut. The tension of his disappointment drew his fists into tight balls.

It had been a long time since he had wanted to release this much steam. He stalked off into the woods, frustrated with his own reaction. Angry at the words that taunted him for caring, for risking his life, for thinking he could make a difference. For thinking a girl like Amy would ever see someone like him as a hero.

Good works might be fine for folks like Joaquin and his uncle, but for him, they'd never be enough. He couldn't do enough good to outweigh the bad he'd done, and what's more, he didn't even get credit when he did the right thing.

Carlos's words came to mind. "When the stakes are high enough, you reveal what you are willing to sacrifice." But what if you sacrifice your heart and still lose?

Amy turned to Joaquin, but he shrugged. What had she said? She realized her half-truth had bothered Slane, but why should he care what she told her parents? He didn't strike her as the boy scout type who would call a half-truth a whole lie.

The rest of them finished their snack in silence and then returned to building the hut. Eventually Slane emerged from the woods and continued to work without a word. Amy's hands grew red and raw from pulling up handfuls of grass, and just as they neared completion, she looked up and saw Laila's mother. The baby was nestled in the bilum bag slung on her back, and a crutch provided by the clinic served more as a walking stick as she poked about for firm ground. Laila and Rayz ran to greet her and help her up the slope. As she approached, favoring her injured leg, her smile spread wide until her face scrunched into smile lines, which made her appear much older than her years. The radiant joy of her smile eclipsed the ache in Amy's back and shoulders.

Tears streamed down Moia's crumpled face, and she grabbed each of them in turn, squeezing their faces and thanking them in Tok Pisin.

"Tenkyu. Tenkyu tru." She repeated it over and over, not believing what she saw.

Amy turned away and blinked back tears of her own. Such a simple thing and yet it had meant everything to this family. She thought for a moment of all the other things she might have done with her time, and nothing compared. The sense of accomplishing something of significance, something of value, for someone who had no means to repay her overwhelmed her with satisfaction. She couldn't imagine any job, any career, any calling which would provide such joy.

She wiped the moisture from her eyes with the back of her dirty hand and caught Slane watching her. Her mind darted back to their earlier conversation. Had she denied Slane the joy she experienced in seeing Moia's appreciation by lying to her parents? She brushed the thought aside and returned to their work, amassing kunai grass for Laila's mother to weave into the mats they would use as beds. A few moments later, she snuck another quick glance his way, but he had returned to tying off bundles of thatch and handing them to Samson.

With the final bundle of thatch secured, Samson swung down from the roof. Joaquin called them all together and pulled out his cell phone to take a picture of the group with the hut in the background. He turned the phone around to show them all the picture. The group looked rough, coated in mud with streaks of sweat cutting through it, but she'd never seen anything more beautiful than the smile on each face.

"Be sure to send me that picture when you get back to Kopi." She poked his arm. "I want to share it with some friends online."

Joaquin agreed and turned to Slane. "We'll have to hurry to make it back before the sun goes down. We should probably get started."

They said goodbye as Laila and her family entered the hut, and her mother sank to the floor, weary from her journey home. Slane and Joaquin walked Amy back to the outpost, their long strides making her jog to keep up. Joaquin tried to start a conversation, but she couldn't keep up her end at the pace they walked, and Slane remained stoic. The sun poised for its final bow as they waved goodbye to her at the gate and hustled to meet Carlos at the clinic for their ride home.

Slane hadn't said another word to her all afternoon. His silence stung more than the tiny cuts the grass had left on her raw hands.

Slane climbed into the chopper beside his friend Joaquin. His friend. The realization caught him off guard. Joaquin was the best friend he had ever had. Perhaps the only real friend he had known. He encouraged Slane, demonstrated forgiveness when Slane screwed up, and called Slane out when he made bad choices.

As Carlos landed at the plantation, and they left the helicopter, Joaquin jolted him out of his thoughts with a jab and broke into a run several steps before calling out, "I'll race you." Slane laughed at the childishness of the moment. They raced down the dirt path like two boys competing for a prize. They could have been anywhere on the planet, but they stood amid lush, emerald mountains and casuarina and areca trees. And suddenly, there was nowhere he'd rather be.

After all their work, their burst of energy quickly waned, and they slowed as they neared the house. Joaquin raised his eyebrows at Slane and spoke through deep inhales to catch his breath. "I caught you watching Amy a few times while we were working."

Slane wondered if the statement hid a question or an accusation. Joaquin made it clear he viewed Amy as a little sister the first night at the singsing, and Slane sensed a protective instinct prompting the observation. With his newfound realization of how rare and precious Joaquin's friendship was to him, he mulled his answer over, trying to avoid offense.

"She's very pretty. But I would never . . . I mean, I know she's like your little sister, so . . . and we're only here for another week, so . . . .." His response didn't sound as reassuring as he'd hoped, but his friend nodded like he understood.

"I'm just giving you a hard time. I am a little protective of her, sure. But I wondered if our work the past several days had provided you with insights beyond the view of a beautiful girl?"

Slane stared at his feet as he thought about it with each step. In his life, he had seen all kinds of deprivation and poverty, but the gratitude of Laila's mother over the hut they'd helped build stunned him. The homeless in Prague camped out in buildings lacking heat and electricity, but at least the concrete structures provided a solid roof and walls. The poor in Santa Cruz scavenged for food in a landfill, but still found many churches and missions nearby to help them.

Laila's family lost everything. Yet they rejoiced over a hut which offered the most basic shelter. The people at the institute stepped in to help, but there were too few of them and too many in need.

The villagers hadn't complained. Hadn't railed against God or wondered why the mudslide happened. Instead, they simply began rebuilding and worked until they finished. He'd watched Samson work almost without pause for several days. Samson would have completed the job alone without their help. It would have taken longer. It might have been more dangerous. But he would have kept working until the family had a home. He had a sense of persistence, determination, and a drive to complete what he'd started. And he'd be back tomorrow working on the next home for someone else.

Slane wondered if he'd ever had the same drive to finish anything. His mind raced home to Prague and all that remained unfinished there for him. The sudden desire to make things right with Mara overwhelmed him. Not to rekindle their relationship, but to admit his failures and ask her forgiveness.

Joaquin still waited for his answer, and Slane had lost track of the question. What had he gotten out of these days of hard work?

He drew his brow together and paused as they reached the house. Holding his friend's attention, he summed it up. "Perspective."

CHAPTER TWELVE

Toby grinned as he brushed his teeth. They had finally cleared the road enough to make travel by foot to Wara safe, or at least almost as safe as it had been before the mudslide. Carlos had brought medicine from the hospital in Mount Hagen back on his last trip, and Toby had convinced his father to let him take it to Miss Maryann. Brandon opted to help with the work of placing gabions to secure the hillside near the road, so his father asked Amy to go with him. She surprised him when she agreed to give up a day helping out on the road with Joaquin and Slane, especially since only a few days of their shore leave remained.

She seemed completely distracted since Slane had arrived. She'd be easy for Toby to ditch. He frowned at the memory of Slane's advice to confess his plans to his father. His sister might be obsessed with the newcomer, but Toby would be glad for him to ship out.

His story to his father had provided a legitimate excuse for all the research he'd been doing. He planned to say he'd spied on the glasman for the paper, too, if he got caught. He had read a bunch of articles about the glasman, and their female counterparts, glasmeri. He'd even read an article claiming they could identify the sanguma, which the writer described as evil spirits inhabiting the bodies of people. The hair on his neck stood on end as he thought of all the terrifying tales he'd read, but the rush of adrenaline the fear brought kept him reading. He knew just because it was on the internet didn't make it true, but he wondered how to know which stories to believe and which were exaggerated or made up altogether.

He glanced at his watch and realized they should have left thirty minutes ago. He let out a frustrated sigh. Amy always made them late. He called out to his sister down the hall.

"Amy, if we don't get started soon, we won't be able to make it to Wara and back before dark."

"Hang on a minute. I'm getting ready to go." Her voice carried from the bedroom.

"What do you need to do to get ready? You don't need makeup or anything." He added a little jab, "You know, Sla-ane isn't going to be there." He stretched the name out just to tease her.

She poked her head out of the room. "Very funny." But her expression revealed annoyance, not amusement. "Just one more minute." She disappeared again, and he stood by the door, trying unsuccessfully to be patient.

When she emerged, they started the long hike to Wara.

They reached the place where the mudslide had taken out the road. Toby saw Carlos's Land Cruiser parked alongside the road and realized the reason for her primping. He should have known. Slane worked beside Joaquin, Brandon, and their father to install the metal cages filled with rocks which would reduce the risk of future landslides.

His sister stopped, and her weak attempt to pretend she needed to talk to her father didn't fool Toby. He stood off to the side, arms folded and avoiding eye-contact with Slane. But Slane seemed to be ignoring him and Amy. He worked hard with his head down and barely glanced up at them.

When Amy eventually realized she wasn't going

to get any attention from the object of her interest, she said goodbye to their father and caught up to where Toby had started up the trail.

As soon as they were out of earshot, Toby asked her, "What is your deal? You are so obvious. Anybody can see you've got it bad for that guy."

She rolled her eyes and frowned at him. "You don't know what you're talking about."

"Oh, yeah. Well, I know he's only here for a few more days. So, you might as well get over it."

She didn't respond. In fact, she ignored him until they reached the bridge.

When Toby took a step onto the bridge, she grabbed his arm. "Are you sure this is safe after the earthquake? What if it falls with us on it?"

They both peered over the edge where the river roared over a cluster of rocks thirty feet below. She had a point. He held onto the rope and tried to shake the bridge. It jiggled a little but seemed secure. He took a couple of steps onto it, still in reach of her arms, and jumped, first a little hop, then a few bigger jumps. Still the bridge remained steady.

"I think it's fine. Come on." He continued across and Amy waited, watching until he had made it across before following him.

Amy clung to the rope as she edged across the bridge. Why? Oh, why had she agreed to go with Toby? The bridge moved under her feet, probably only millimeters, but it felt as if it swayed back and forth under her unsteady legs. Fear escaped her lips in a whimper.

Toby had made it to the far side and urged her on.

"Come on, Amy. The bridge is fine! Stop being such a baby!" The desire to mete out a little sisterly retribution motivated her and kept her moving until she reached solid land once more.

"Now who's the baby?" She punched him in the arm and immediately regretted it. He was unfazed, and her knuckles cracked painfully.

"Are you done? Can we go now?" He didn't wait for an answer but set out up the narrow trail through the woods.

Amy spent the rest of their journey pondering the answer to Toby's question about her interest in Slane. She wasn't about to tell her little brother Slane had literally saved her life two days ago. She hadn't told anyone and hoped Laila wouldn't either. But Slane had captured her attention long before he saved her from the mudslide.

The image of Slane and Joaquin working on the road beside her father flashed through her mind. She hadn't even thought about one of them letting the story slip. Of course, she hadn't asked them not to tell, but she had told them she had concealed it.

The expression on Slane's face when she explained her pretext haunted her, as if she had crushed him in some way she didn't understand. In fact, she didn't know why she hadn't told her parents the whole truth. She tried to convince herself that her concern over them worrying provided enough justification.

But she knew in her heart there was more to it.

She enjoyed guarding a secret.

Something else nagged at her as well. She couldn't put her finger on it, but she felt like she knew Slane. Something teased her memory about his tall, lanky frame, the shock of hair which hung in his eyes until he tossed it aside with a jerk of his head, the piercing stare suggesting interest yet with an intensity hinting at danger.

She shook her head. What was it about him? Why couldn't she get him out of her head? Why did his unusual name ring so familiar? And what would she do in a few days when he and Joaquin returned to Port Moresby, and from there to who-knows-where?

She'd never see him again once he left Haedi. The thought brought both a rush of relief and a painful void.

Lost in thought, she barely noticed how quickly the trek went. They entered the village, and, after spending two days constructing a home for her friend, Amy marveled at the differences between the two types of homes. Laila's home, and the other homes in Haedi, were circular, with a dirt floor and pieces of bush wood comprising the walls.

In Wara, they built rectangular homes, raised off the ground, with steeply-pitched roofs. They wove bamboo into walls which allowed the mountain breezes to keep them cool. Patterns woven into the walls added to the beauty of the village. The roofs in Wara were also thatch, but some of them had sprouted and vines and greenery grew out of the roof almost covering the entire home. The smoke from cookfires burning inside filtered through the thatch and rose over the village, giving it a mystical appeal, like a fairytale land enveloped in the clouds.

As she admired the simple appeal of the village, an elderly man appeared at the door of his hut and startled her. His appearance would startle anyone who had become accustomed to the villagers in Haedi where they followed more Western styles.

She immediately recognized the village glasman.

His only clothing was a loin cloth, but tattoos and traditional jewelry fashioned from rough cut stones, animal teeth, and bones covered his torso. His headdress rose a foot above his head, covered in feathers from the brightly colored parrots native to the area. Long, curved pig tusks protruded from piercings on either side of his nose.

Amy jumped as he scurried down from his hut and approached them, shrieking in her face in a language she'd never heard. Toby grabbed her arm and pulled her toward Miss Maryann's home. The man stood with his feet planted and arms raised, watching them, and shouting as they fled.

Slane paused from hefting large rocks into the gabions and wiped his brow as he gazed up the path Amy had taken. Joaquin had been right. He had more than a passing interest in the girl, but he had little hope. She was the daughter of a missionary, and he was a homeless, worthless son of an even more worthless, no-good criminal. Good thing they'd be leaving in two days. It would be the best thing all around.

He picked up the next rock and the next. If it was the best thing all around, why was it so hard?

Amy's father had paused as well. Slane glanced toward the older man and caught his eyes on him. Smiling to break the tension, he tried to think of something to say.

"Your son Toby is quite an explorer."

The father smiled and returned to the work of stacking the gabions against the hillside. He responded after a few moments, as if making casual conversation. "What makes you think so?"

Slane hesitated. He didn't want to betray the boy's confidence, but now he had started an exchange and he searched for a truthful answer.

"He, um, just told me about how much he likes making the trek up to the village." He jerked his head in the direction they'd taken. "Apparently it's a pretty intense hike." Man, he wished he had never opened his big mouth. His voice squeaked like a mouse and sounded for all the world like he'd lied through his teeth.

"Really." The father kept working for several minutes and then paused again. "What did he tell you?"

Slane had never felt any particular compunction to tell the truth, but in this moment, he felt pinned to a wall and dosed with truth serum. As Toby's father made eye-contact, Slane searched his imagination and found no lie to satisfy the man. Nothing came to mind except the facts, and they came spilling out.

"He found a bone near the trail. A human bone, he thinks. And he's been spying on someone he called the glasman. He acted kind of obsessed with the whole thing. He was really intent on investigating where the bone came from and whether the glasman had anything to do with it. I tried to convince him to tell you about it. Honestly, I did."

The man's face had lost a shade of color, and Slane wondered how a simple question had prompted him to spill Toby's secret.

"When did he tell you this?"

Slane wondered if the set jaw and the slight tic near his eye conveyed worry or anger, but he knew he had to tell him everything now.

"It was the first day, the day of the mudslide. He

said something about having returned to where he found the bone and finding a skull, too. He said the last time he spied on the glasman; the man saw him."

A shout from Samson interrupted their conversation as the man they had pulled from the debris a few days earlier ran toward them shouting frantically. Toby's father turned as Samson pulled the survivor forward. "Nizax, tell him what happened."

"All of Wara is in an uproar! The glasman told the people a witch is causing illness and death."

Samson added, "Who? Who is he accusing this time?"

"The missionary woman, Maryann. I tried to warn her she must leave, but she would not listen to me. You must go and tell her."

"Maryann has lived in Wara for years. They know she is a Christian, not a witch."

Nizax blurted out, "She stood up to the glasman when he accused Moia of sanguma. She led the people who believe in God and told them they must not let Moia be killed. They stood together against the glasman to save her and send her away." He seemed stricken with guilt. "I told them I had found Moia and her family in Haedi and about the landslide. I thought when the people heard how I had been saved by the God the missionary speaks of, they would understand and no longer believe the glasman." He paused for a moment as tears slid down his face. "But the glasman told them the landslide destroyed Haedi because the sprites became angry at this village for welcoming a witch. He says Maryann saved Moia because she is the mother of the witches."

All eyes locked on Nizax as fear took hold. Slane's throat constricted as he thought of Amy and Toby walking into a dangerous trap.

Her father barked orders like an Army general, starting with Joaquin. "We need your uncle's helicopter, Joaquin. He knows where Wara is. Get there as fast as you can."

Joaquin ran for the Land Cruiser and spun mud from the tires as he raced toward Kopi.

"Iatmul, run to the clinic and let them know what has happened. They need to be prepared." Iatmul turned and ran back toward the outpost. Slane's blood ran cold imagining what they needed to prepare for.

No one questioned or hesitated. Amy's father led the way, with Brandon, Elsen, Nizax, and Samson following. Slane barely kept pace as they raced up the path Amy and Toby had taken a few hours earlier.

CHAPTER THIRTEEN

Slane caught sight of the footbridges, and his stomach lurched into his throat. They were little more than ropes stringing together scraps of wood and bamboo across the deep gorge with a narrow island in the middle. A large block of poured concrete secured each end of the bridge. Amy's father started across without hesitation. He continued past the landing onto the second bridge. As the others followed him and the bridge swayed under the weight of five grown men, Slane saw the frayed rope on the far end snaking through the connector on the concrete anchorage. He shouted a warning.

"The bridge! It's coming loose!"

Amy's father glanced at the anchorage and raced to the end, the other four close behind. The rope held but appeared it might give way at any moment.

"Slane, don't take a chance!" Amy's father cupped his hands around his mouth and shouted over the sound of rushing water at the bottom of the gorge. "Go back and wait at Haedi."

Carlos's words echoed in his mind. "When the stakes are high, we reveal what we are willing to sacrifice." He took a deep breath and raced onto the bridge, even as the others hollered, "No!"

His long legs carried him quickly across the bridge. With just two strides left, the rope snapped. As if in slow motion, the bridge pulled loose and began to fall. He launched himself forward as the planks under his feet gave way, and he hit the concrete anchorage hard. The impact knocked the breath from his lungs, and his fingers clawed at the loose dirt as the men grabbed his arms and dragged him up to where they stood.

Amy's father stared at him for a moment, his expression unreadable. Slane brushed off the dirt and met his gaze without backing down. "Let's go."

As soon as Maryann opened the door, Toby filled her in. "What is up with the glasman? He's never said anything to us before, but when he saw us coming in to the village, he started yelling and waving his arms. I don't know what he said, but he really freaked Amy out." His sister leaned against the wall with a stunned expression.

"I wish we could stay and visit, but maybe we should just leave." He pulled the medicine from his backpack and handed it to her. "I don't know what made him so angry, but we must have done something he didn't like." He glanced toward the door. He wondered if his spying had angered the glasman.

"It isn't you." Maryann patted Toby's shoulder. "He has grown more and more agitated lately. Many of the people in the village have believed in Christ and are reading the Bible in their own language, or at least the portion we've translated so far. They've turned away from the beliefs of previous generations, and especially beliefs in the glasman's ability to heal them. Then Nizax returned and told how God rescued him from the landslide, and even more villagers wanted to know about God and put their faith in Him."

"What does any of this have to do with us?" Amy's voice sounded tiny and afraid.

"The glasman is losing his position of honor and

power among the people. They no longer turn to him; they turn instead to God. And, in his view, all of us are to blame because we bring the gospel." Maryann stepped to the door and peeked out through a crack before turning back to them.

"He's threatened a few times, but he always backed down before it got too serious. I knew what had happened in the past when he accused a woman of sanguma, but I had never seen it happening. When he accused Moia, I had to step in and stop them from hurting her. I gathered all those who had placed their faith in Christ, and we stood against him. The people literally stood between him and Moia while I freed her and led her and her children down the mountain to Haedi. I knew the glasman would be furious, but he backed down when the people stood up to him. He has been stirring up such anger and fear.

"When Nizax brought news of the earthquake and mudslide, he told everyone Moia and her family survived the landslide in Haedi. He thought when they saw how God had protected her, it would strengthen their faith. But the glasman called it witchcraft and told them supernatural forces had punished Haedi for harboring Moia, a witch. "

She peeked again through the crack and drew a sharp breath. "He has a group of men with him, and more coming to join them, but I can't hear what he is telling them. They burned the ceremonial fires all through the night last night. They've never done that before."

Toby had never seen the elderly missionary anxious. But now fear wrinkled her brow, her trembling hands clasped each other, and her voice quivered. As her eyes darted over the two of them, he realized she feared for him and his sister, not for herself. Amy slid down the wall. The color in her cheeks from the hike up the mountain had vanished, leaving her skin almost translucent.

"Why don't we slip out the back like we're going to the liklik haus?" Toby moved toward the back of the hut, where a small door led to the path to her outhouse.

Maryann checked the village field again and shook her head. "I don't think we would get very far without them finding us. He has too many people with him now. And they keep pointing this way."

Shouts from outside sent a chill down Toby's spine. Did he want to know what the words meant? Maybe not. Then a loud voice raised above the others.

The hint of a smile crept to Maryann's watered eyes. "It's one of the leaders of the tribe. I've been teaching him to read the excerpts of the Bible we have translated to their language. He's saying I've only helped them." She paused, and Toby heard the glasman's raised voice but didn't understand him. Maryann continued, "But the glasman says following God as I've taught them has angered the sprites and made them stop cooperating with him. They no longer show him the cause of illness in the village."

Had the glasman moved closer to the hut or was he just shouting louder? Toby sank to the floor beside Amy and wrapped an arm around her shivering shoulders.

The proximity of the voices became more evident now. They were close. They roared in an angry cadence and the thin, woven bamboo walls of the hut provided no defense. Maryann backed away from the doorway, coming to sit with them in a huddle.

She prayed earnestly, and Toby listened and whispered amen as she pleaded with the Lord for their safety and for the salvation of her neighbors.

Amy's mind raced through all the trauma of the past days. Her body trembled. The roar of the landslide echoed in the crowd's tumult. The chill of the mud engulfing her returned in the cold that gripped her now. Her pulse raced as her breathing came in short, quick gasps.

The room spiraled and dimmed as her view shifted. Her perspective pivoted back upon herself, and she watched her body shaking, saw her own eyes wide and dilated. Her consciousness rose to a spot where she hovered near the top of the hut. She seemed so small, hunkered down with her younger brother's arm around her like a tiny child. A part of her brain rationally analyzed the situation and recognized the physical signs of shock. Her rapid breathing and heartbeat failed to provide enough oxygen to her brain, and she would soon lose consciousness. She'd heard fear gives a fight-or-flight response, but her response seemed to be to shut down. To insulate herself against the chaos around her by disconnecting herself from it.

Like a nightmare where her feet refused to move, paralysis held her captive.

The raging voices outside combined with drums into a thunderous rumble until she couldn't distinguish words from drumbeats. The mob roared like a living beast, intent on devouring them, gnashing its teeth and pounding the drums of death at the door of the hut. Amy had never given thought to the powerful nature of spiritual warfare, but now she understood it clearly.

Maryann's prayer broke through the cocoon of Amy's shock and fear.

"Father, we are in your hands and trusting in your mercy. You know our greatest desire is for our neighbors and friends to know you. If you call us to lay down our lives for the sake of them coming to know you, we are willing to do it. But Lord, it is hard to imagine how this could be your plan." She sniffled, and her voice broke. Amy watched herself below, shaking and pale, her fingers folded together and tinged faintly blue. Maryann continued, "Father, help us be courageous in the face of evil. Most of all, protect these children!" Without another word, Miss Maryann pulled herself out of their embrace and walked to the door, throwing it wide.

Maryann stood in the doorway and confronted the glasman.

"If you want me, here I am!" she shouted in his face, her toes literally lined up with his bare feet, and her chin set. The fear which had consumed her a moment before vanished without a trace. "But you will not hurt these children." She nodded toward them and continued to stand in the doorway, blocking entrance to the hut.

The glasman grinned through the paint covering his face, and Amy shuddered at his broken teeth, stained blood-red from the betel nuts he chewed. He grabbed the brave saint and dragged her from the doorway to the village center. As he did, he shouted over his shoulder, and two other tribesmen entered the hut and grabbed Toby and Amy, pulling them out as well.

Slane marveled at the older man's stamina. They sprinted up the steep slope, and Amy's father showed no signs of being winded, while Slane gasped for air.

"I've got to catch . . . my breath . . . " He slowed to a walk and sucked in the thin air fast enough to keep moving. Amy's father's pace never wavered. If it weren't for Slane's long legs, he would have lost sight of the older man. Elsen and Samson had already fallen behind fifty yards. Brandon slowed and came alongside him.

Slane hated to ask, but he had to know what they might face. "I'm not sure I understand. What will they do if the glasman claims the missionary is a witch?"

"We've heard stories about glasmen accusing someone, usually a woman, of being a sanguma—a witch. Practicing sorcery." Brandon answered.

Slane nodded, and they increased pace again to a jog to keep Amy's father in sight as her brother explained.

"The bones Toby found. They may be evidence this happens even in our region." They jogged several more steps, with Slane still trying to comprehend. "A few months ago, the glasman accused Laila's mother of witchcraft. Miss Maryann rescued her and helped her escape, wrecking the glasman's plan."

Amy's father must have overheard the conversation. He called over his shoulder through tight lips, "If the glasman decides Maryann, or even Toby or Amy, are guilty of sorcery, he has the power in the tribe to order their torture and execution."

Slane stumbled. Torture and execution? Surely, he was just being an overprotective father.

He responded as though he'd heard Slane's thoughts.

"I'm not overreacting. They aren't just stories. There have been hundreds of cases in the past year alone. The number is up for the third year in a row."

"I don't understand. How could he accuse them of witchcraft? It doesn't make any sense if they're Christians. I don't know much about Christians, but I thought they were opposed to witchcraft."

Amy's father continued, "They make these accusations for all sorts of reasons. Sometimes it's because someone in the village has died, and the people don't understand the cause. They can't see infections or diseases. It's easier to blame a person, to say this person is the one causing anything bad the village experiences. Sometimes it's as simple as greed. Someone wants land or possessions. They use the glasman or glasmeri to put an end to the one who stands in their way and then claim the property for themselves."

Slane's mind flashed to the brutality of gangs in his home and to his own suffering at the hands of human traffickers. The same evil stretched from one end of the globe to the other, reaching even this remote island nation. Even their isolation from other cultures for thousands of years hadn't kept them from learning cruelty, abuse, and violence. It seemed to him each human being carried within them the capacity for such evil.

They pressed on in silence. The urgency now clearly painted for each of them. Slane's mind raced through the possibility they would be too late. Images from his own experience with torture haunted him as they ran. He tried to drive away the memories, but even the wild beauty surrounding him failed to distract him from the horror of what they might find when they reached Wara.

As the sunlight flashed through the trees, Amy's face came to mind. With the next step, Mara's face flashed before him. Each step brought another face from his memory, a rapid-fire slideshow of pain and suffering. Some he'd helped to torment, others he'd stood by and allowed it to happen. Still others had loomed over him as his recollections rolled back to the time when he was the victim.

This thing, this virulent strain driving human beings to such senseless acts of cruelty, whatever the disease, it infected him just as it did those who threatened Toby and Amy now.

He had justified his own violence because it was all he'd ever known. From his father to the criminals who had kidnapped him in Prague, to a long line of others leading to this moment, he'd experienced his own share of abuse. He'd seen the darkness which lurked inside, bided its time, and then raged in fury the moment it escaped the leash.

But along the way, the victim had overcome his abusers by becoming the oppressor. The weak had become strong, but not just strong—cruel. Unfeeling. Willing to do anything to achieve his goals.

Every thump of his feet on the ground felt like a drum beating the words into his skull: guil-ty. Guil-ty. GUIL-TY.

But the pounding he heard wasn't his feet. They neared the village, and the drums hammered out a rhythm which set them all racing against time.

Smoke curled among the trees with an acrid stench rather than the pleasant aroma of cook fires. Slane's heart lurched like something had wrenched it loose in his chest. One minute it rose into his throat like a knot choking off his oxygen; the next moment it plummeted to his gut and made him fight the urge to retch. He raced ahead, leading the way as the first huts came into view.

CHAPTER FOURTEEN

Toby stumbled as the men dragged him and his sister to the center of the field. He stood before the villagers, his mouth hanging open as the glasman gripped Amy's arm in one hand and Miss Maryann's arm in the other.

The glasman shouted and gestured at the three of them.

"He said—" Miss Maryann began to translate for Toby and Amy, but Toby cut her off.

"I understood him!" Toby comprehended the meaning even though he'd never heard the words before as the glasman continued.

"These spirit women have come and taught you to abandon the sprites who helped us and our fathers and their fathers for many generations to heal the sick. Now the sprites no longer speak to me or show me the cause of your disease because of them. They are teaching you to follow her god and to listen to his spirit instead of honoring the sprites."

Toby tried to make eye contact with Amy, but she stared with vacant eyes. Her face lacked any emotion, the muscles slack as if she slept. Her skin glowed a translucent white like a ghostly apparition.

The villagers encircled them, and their faces bore a mixture of fear and confusion. The glasman continued to build his case against them, speaking directly to his people.

"You all have known since you were small children that each person possesses a big soul and a little soul. The big soul leads us in all good things. Kindness. Generosity. Love." Sharp gestures punctuated each sentence. The glasman paused the rant for a moment, and the people leaned in, intent on every word. When he resumed, his volume increased and his arms flailed as his eyes grew wild.

"But the small soul seeks only selfish things. This small soul is with us always, but the big soul travels away from our body in our dreams." He waved his arms, mimicking a bird soaring in the sky. "It visits far-off places and explores worlds we cannot see when we are awake. It speaks to sprites and learns all that is needed for healing." He paused again, and the people in the circle nodded. His description echoed the folklore Toby had read; stories and beliefs which existed generations before the missionaries came.

The glasman continued, "But since this woman came," he shook Maryann hard, like Bublé might shake a stuffed toy, "the little soul in me is all I have. The big soul in me can no longer seek the sprites. The sprites no longer share their wisdom with me so I can share it with you and heal you."

Toby saw the anxiety on the faces around the circle. They had depended on the glasman's healing all their lives.

"You all know how witchcraft and sorcery, sanguma, are spreading everywhere. The ringleaders of sorcery may say they serve God, but really, they help the sanguma people. I tried to protect you by destroying the witch among us, but this one stood in our way. You all saw," he pointed to the people surrounding him, "how she kept us from killing the sanguma before. She is on the side of sorcery! She is the queen of the witches!"

Some of the villagers roared in support, and the glasman fed off their enthusiasm. Others shifted their gazes to the ground and backed toward the outer edges of the crowd. "Our people are dying because this woman has come and brought with her the spirit of her god to replace our spirits. Her spirit has become powerful, and we must kill her to rid our village of this evil."

Those who had cheered around the circle nodded and shook their fists in the air, clasping spears or stone axes. The ones on the outskirts appeared as frightened and confused as his sister. Emboldened, the glasman continued his tirade, shaking Amy like a rag doll as he spoke. "Now she has brought this one. And with her, the ground shakes and the mountain falls. The sprites sent judgment on them by causing the ground to swallow the village where they tried to hide the witch. If we do not put an end to them, the sprites will bring destruction on our village as well."

Now he directed his gaze at Toby, pointing a gnarled finger in his direction. "And this one is guilty, too! He spied on me as I called to the sprites for healing. He wants to steal them from us! They are evil, and their evil is too powerful! We must save our village from all of them!"

The people's expressions ranged from wide-eyed, anxious glances to fierce anger.

One of the men shouted, and Toby understood every word even though he didn't speak their language. "The landslide buried our family members. We have heard about the village at Haedi, near where the other missionaries live." He held one hand palm up and swept his other palm against it as if wiping a table clean. "How the landslide wiped it out." With their pain still raw, the glasman had provided a villain to blame for their loss.

Beside him, a man began chanting for vengeance against them. Toby's heart raced, and he searched for something, anything, to stop the growing tide of anger and violence.

A stirring in the crowd drew his eyes to the commotion as his father, Nizax, Slane, and several of the men from Haedi entered the circle. Nizax, the man they had rescued from the mudslide, pushed his way to the front and shouted over the chaos.

"You heard what the glasman said. He only has the little soul in him now. We who have believed in Jesus and follow Him know what this little soul is. It is the enemy who wants to destroy each of us. It is the part of ourselves leading us to turn away from all God has for us and to follow our own ideas. Our own selfish pursuits."

Nizax pointed at the glasman, and Toby stood in wonder at his own understanding. Like the glasman, Nizax spoke in their tribal language. Toby knew many in the village did not speak English, and he didn't speak their tongue, yet he'd understood the glasman and the other villager. Now he listened intently as Nizax countered the tribe's leader.

"The glasman has given himself over to the little soul, to the part of himself that is evil. He no longer hears the Big Soul, because every good intention we have comes from the Spirit of God. The glasman has rejected the Big Soul, the Spirit of God, and is consumed with evil."

Nizax stepped toward Amy and Maryann. "But when we follow Jesus, we do not do what is evil any longer. We all saw when the Big Soul gave our friend the courage," he put his arm around Maryann's shoulders, "to stand up and protect the innocent. Those who stood with her and helped Moia and her children escape obeyed the Spirit of God who loves all people." He swept his other hand toward Toby's father and the others. "I've seen this Spirit in these people as they worked and sacrificed to help the people of Haedi. When the mud buried me, I saw the One they call Jesus, and He saved me."

Amy's bird's eye view of herself continued as the glasman shouted, his eyes wild and terrifying, but she didn't understand him. Nizax, the man Laila's parents had committed her to marry, stepped into the circle. Amy couldn't understand what he said any more than she understood the glasman.

She shivered, and the scene below faded like a cloud passing between her vision and the activity below.

Her hands and face chilled as though it was winter in the Midwest rather than summer in the tropics, but a warmth oozed over the back of her head. She turned toward the source of the heat. She wondered if she might get too close to the sun as the scene below grew distant and hazy. But instead of the sun, she saw a figure, glowing bright as the sun. She couldn't make out his features, but she knew, deep inside, that Jesus stood before her. The warmth drew her in, and she longed to rush into his arms. But the figure below, the small blonde girl standing in the circle, held her back. An anchor bound her to that person who now seemed almost a stranger to her.

She wanted to cast the anchor away. It was dead weight. A burden. Her true life belonged here in the warmth of Jesus's presence. Below stood only a frail tent of flesh which had housed her for a season.

But even as she tried to pull away from the girl below, she sensed Him telling her to be patient. To wait. Her time to spend eternity with Him would come, but for now, she had more work to do.

All her fears about insignificance, all her desires to make a difference, all her discontentment with her life were laid bare before Him, and He wiped them away. He whispered in her heart, "Well done, good and faithful servant. These words are not for what you will do, but for what I have already done. Your significance is not based on you accomplishing great things in my Name, but in you resting in what my Name has already accomplished in you. Go, return, and walk in the works I created for you to do."

The words were barely uttered when her perspective shifted instantaneously. She stood in the midst of the village beside Maryann and peered around her at the circle of faces. The vision of her Savior had dissolved into sight of the glasman on the ground with Toby kneeling beside him, both in tears. She felt the absence of Jesus's physical presence like a gaping wound, yet a newfound resolve grew in her heart.

Nizax's voice rang out clearly, articulately, resounding in the village as the glasman seemed to melt before him. But now she understood his words as clearly as the villagers did.

Toby trembled at the realization he had allowed his curiosity, his obsession with the mysterious glasman, to drown the voice of God in his life. Just like the glasman, he had followed the little soul, rather than the Spirit of God.

"Many of you have said you want to follow Jesus. But when you put your trust in Jesus, you must let go of selfish desires." Nizax's words held a mirror before Toby's soul. He had pursued his curiosity even when he knew it was leading him away from God. "The little soul still lives in you, and in me. In all of us. When you follow Jesus, that little soul must die. We must put all the selfishness and evil of the little soul to death every single day, and we must be led by the Big Soul, the Holy Spirit."

The glasman let go of Toby's sister and Miss Maryann and dropped to the ground, his face contorting in grief. Were the words penetrating his heart as they had Toby's? The glasman pleaded for mercy and forgiveness. Despite the fear which had consumed Toby moments before, compassion for the man and the desire to see him reconciled to God eclipsed his fear. In his own obsession, he was no different than the glasman. He had elevated his curiosity above everything — his relationship with his family, his integrity, and even above God.

The glasman sobbed and cried out, "Please! Put to death this little soul of envy and bitterness! Give to me the Big Soul, the Holy Spirit. Let me not be consumed with hatred and violence, but fill me with this joy you speak of, the joy of salvation. Help me!"

Toby heard and understood the words of the glasman and marveled at their source. How could a man intent on murder a moment ago be so overcome by grief and repentance now? How had he pivoted from his passion for the mysterious occult practices to this realization of his own need for forgiveness and grace?

He listened as Nizax continued to share the gospel. "I have no power to do this. It is not me you need. Jesus has already done all you need to free you from the evil one. You must put your trust in Him and what He has done. Each of us must seek to let Him work in us daily. We must believe with faith that He will do what He has said He would do."

"Yes! Yes!" the man cried out and clung to Toby like his life depended upon it. Toby felt hot tears burning his cheeks. He was as guilty as the groveling man beside him.

"And if you believe, Jesus said you proclaim your faith to others by being baptized. It is a picture of putting the little soul to death and raising from the dead with the Big Soul, the Holy Spirit, to guide you."

Toby's father knelt beside them. As his father met his gaze, Toby confessed, "Dad, I'm so sorry! I lied, and I hid things from you. I only cared about my own foolish curiosity and didn't care who I hurt. I believed in Jesus, but I didn't obey Him as Lord. I didn't let the Holy Spirit guide me, but trusted and pursued in my own imagination instead."

His father rested one hand on the old man's head and the other on Toby's and prayed over them.

"Father, we thank You for how You have worked in these lives today. Thank You for protecting those we love, but thank You even more for demonstrating Your love and kindness to us all once again by extending Your saving grace. Thank You for giving them both the precious gift of sincere repentance and comforting them as they see their sin exactly as You see it. Give them strength to turn to You for everything, but especially for healing. In the matchless Name of Jesus, we pray, Amen."

The glasman raised his tear-streaked face and embraced them both. Toby's sister and Maryann joined them and Brandon, Elsen, and Samson crowded in as well. Someone began singing a hymn in the tribal tongue, and the voices blended together in two languages. He tried to wrap his mind around what had happened. They'd been about to die. Amy and Maryann had been about to be abused and murdered. But God had stepped in.

God had spoken to them both through a man who had been all but dead when they found him days ago, buried in the mud. From death to life, from ashes to beauty, God had worked miracle after miracle, leading to this moment. The sun burst through the clouds and turned the circle of believers into a golden crown of light.

Slane stood silently and watched the group as the song filled the village. He didn't know the words or the tune.

The bizarre events he'd just witnessed replayed in his mind. He'd surged ahead at the sight of the old man, covered in mud and paint, tusks protruding from his nostrils, the gnarled fingers of one hand gripping Amy's biceps. His gut instinct screamed for him to attack the man. He towered more than a foot taller and had at least thirty pounds of muscular advantage on the wiry man. It would all be over in a moment, and he would be the hero.

But Amy's father had seized him, immobilizing him in a bear hug for a moment that stretched into an epic battle in his own mind.

A voice raged inside him, "This isn't your fight! These aren't your people! You don't even believe their Christian nonsense. You should turn around and leave before it's too late." His eyes had darted from Amy's father and older brother, then to Toby, then rested on Amy.

A conviction arose in the pit of his stomach. This was a moment of truth for him. For his soul. Carlos had challenged him to think about what he was willing to risk, but Amy's father had held him back when he would have risked his own life to save her. What if risking it all meant a spiritual sacrifice, rather than a physical one?

He didn't have an answer to that question, but when Amy's father had released him, his feet felt nailed to the spot.

Then Nizax, the man they'd pulled from the wreckage of the village, stood in the midst of the angry mob. He shouted in a language Slane didn't understand. The people listened, and their expressions softened almost imperceptibly.

Whatever the man said, even the painted man holding the women captive had been mesmerized. The glasman's gaze had locked onto Nizax, and the man seemed to transform in front of them.

The glasman's hands relaxed and fell to his sides, leaving a purple bruise on the pale skin of Amy's arm. The old man dropped to his knees slowly, the muscles in his legs melting. He wept, crying out in pleas for mercy. His body spoke a universal language of brokenness as he fell forward onto his face in the dirt. He groveled and writhed as if an alien might emerge from his gut, and Slane wouldn't have been surprised after all he'd seen.

Toby knelt beside the painted man and spoke quietly as tears flooded his face. His father came and laid hands on their heads in a gesture so kind and loving Slane felt like he was eavesdropping on a moment of sacred intimacy.

The glasman, lying prostrate in the dirt, seemed pathetic and degrading; yet a part of Slane envied the man for the transformation unfolding in this moment.

What had Nizax said? How had he performed such a miraculous metamorphosis in someone who had been ready to kill them seconds before? Slane wanted to rush in, to ask questions, to figure out what he had just witnessed, but his feet stood rooted to the spot.

Overhead, the thwak-thwak-thwak of the helicopter rotor proclaimed that Joaquin and Carlos had arrived, and the moment of decision passed.

CHAPTER FIFTEEN

By the time Carlos shuttled them all back to Haedi Outpost, the sun had set. Amy hadn't even had the energy to eat when they got home but rinsed the grime of the day off with a quick shower and fell into bed exhausted. As the sun peeked through her window, she woke to the sounds of her family preparing for church.

"Hurry up, sweetie," her mom's voice called from the kitchen. "It's almost time to go."

Today, Laila would be baptized following the church service! Prompted by the memory, Amy popped up and threw on a meri blause and wrap skirt and slid her feet into sandals. She pulled a brush through her hair and stepped into the bathroom to brush her teeth and run a washcloth over her face. As she walked through the kitchen, she grabbed a few slices of mango and followed her family out the door.

The walk across the outpost to church seemed quieter than most Sundays. Ruth clung to her mom's hand instead of running ahead. Toby followed them, and her dad walked beside him, a little closer than usual, it seemed. Brandon lagged behind her a few steps. Amy reflected on how Laila had come to faith, how she had immediately shared the story with Moia, and how Moia had been saved. Meanwhile, Amy had buried the details of their miraculous rescue. Her heart ached with the weight of her secret.

They were halfway to the church when Toby broke the silence.

"Dad, I should have told you the truth when I found the bone. I got so caught up in the mystery of it,

I didn't see how it took my attention away from everything else, even God. I just never thought keeping a secret could cause so much trouble. When Nizax spoke to the glasman yesterday, I understood everything he said. It made me realize I am no better than the glasman." He shuffled his feet, kicking up a little cloud of dust.

"Toby, it's amazing that God allowed you to understand, kind of like when Peter preached at Pentecost. God has a way of getting our attention when we are wandering from Him. We often think we can handle difficult problems on our own, but God gives us family and friends to help us. We aren't alone, and we shouldn't disregard the support of our community." Her father rested a hand on her brother's shoulder.

Amy's own secret weighed heavily on her mind. Her dad asked Toby, "What do you feel like you need to do now that you've realized your mistake?"

Toby shuffled along for several steps before responding. "Well, the first thing was to confess. So I've done that. I told you about it." Her dad nodded.

"And then try to make it right, I guess. But how do I make it right?"

Her father smiled, but it didn't reach his eyes. "Sometimes we can't undo the mistake we've made. Makes it all the more important to learn from it, right?" Toby nodded, and Amy's stomach clenched.

They'd arrived at the steps to the church, and the first strains of music greeted them. Too late for her to confess her own secret. She went through the motions during the service, her heart too burdened by guilt to offer sincere worship. The sight of Slane standing with Joaquin, Carlos, and Gloria near the front distracted her even more.

As the pastor dismissed them, he invited all those who had placed their faith in Jesus to follow them down to the spring where they baptized new believers.

Amy left the church with her family and searched the crowd for her friend Laila, even as she sensed Slane's eyes boring into her back. She cast a quick glance over her shoulder but didn't see him. Maybe she imagined it.

The congregation followed the pastor down the hill to an area where a natural spring formed a pond. She craned her neck still trying to catch sight of her friend in the group. Leaves and debris from the recent rains polluted the muddy water, but the pastor stepped down into it as if it were a crystal clear pool.

One by one, believers joined him, declared their faith before the congregation, and rose from the murky water as new creations. The contrast of the disgusting water and the radiance on their faces made the moment more compelling. The crowd whooped and cheered as each person emerged from the water.

Finally, Amy saw Laila approaching the pool. Behind her, Moia and Nizax had also lined up for baptism. Laila stepped into the watering hole and shouted, "I believe Jesus has done everything to save me, and I will follow Him wherever He leads!" The pastor placed one hand on the hands she'd folded across her chest and one on her back as he swept her under the water and back up in one smooth motion. "I baptize you, my sister, in the name of the Father, the Son, and the Holy Spirit!"

Laila slogged out of the water and cheered as her mother and Nizax were baptized. After hugging them both in wet, muddy embraces, she rushed over to Amy, still dripping, and wrapped her in a sloppy hug.

Nizax trailed behind her, along with her mother and siblings.

"I'm so excited for you, my sister." Amy's spirit lifted at the joy on her friend's face.

"God has already answered so many prayers for me and for Mami." Laila smiled and gestured toward her family. "Nizax has promised to help us stay in Haedi. He told me this morning about the glasman, and how he found repentance. But he agreed it will be better for us to be here. He wants to stay in Haedi and learn more about God and study at the outpost to be able to teach the people. He said if it is God's will for us to marry, we will both know it is right when it is time."

They were safe. Laila and her family could live in their new home in peace and safety. God had done more than Amy had asked or imagined. But her heart grieved over her failure to own up to the truth.

By the time the last person had been baptized, the crowd had thinned and Amy and her father walked home alone. The secret had gnawed at her all morning and refused to wait any longer.

"Dad, I need to tell you something. After yesterday, I realized I shouldn't be keeping secrets from you and Mom."

Her father met her gaze, and she read the array of emotions flitting across his expression. He nodded slowly, preparing himself for anything.

"The other day, when I came home covered in mud, I didn't tell you the whole truth about what happened."

He took a deep breath but waited for her to finish.

"I was trying to help Laila gather wood for their house. And I ended up falling into the sludge and debris from the mudslide." She raced on with the story, eager to unburden her conscience. "I sank up to my neck in the stuff, and I thought I was going to die. Laila came and tried to save me, and then she fell in, too; and Slane and Joaquin came and saved us. Slane literally saved my life." She paused for a second and then continued without waiting for his reaction. She felt the weight of conviction lifting as she confessed. "And then, when I told him and Joaquin I had made up a story about how I got so muddy, he just shut down. He hasn't spoken to me since. Even yesterday, he kept his distance. He didn't even speak to me. I'm surprised he even bothered to come with you to Wara. Honestly, I bet he wishes he left my ungrateful self in the mud." Tears welled up. "Dad, I know I shouldn't have lied, and it really hurt him. But I don't know how to fix it."

Her father's eyes widened as she spoke, and it took a moment before he spoke. "Amy, I can tell you he didn't wish he had left you there. I don't know if you can fix this or not, but you need to apologize. And you don't have much time. I spoke to Carlos this morning, and he said he wouldn't be able to transport any patients today because he is taking Joaquin and Slane back to POM after church today. The captain of the ship messaged them, and the repairs are completed."

"What?" With all the work rebuilding the village, she'd lost track of the days, but she thought they had several more days. Now their shore leave had been cut short. "Dad, you've got to take me to Kopi! I have to try to catch them before they leave."

She raced up the hill and across the outpost to their home with her dad following her. He cranked the Kawasaki Mule, and she hopped in. The little 4X4 zipped over the unpaved roads and past the gate of the institute. The repairs to the road had created a single lane of traffic, and the temporary shutdown had resulted in more vehicles than usual when it finally opened. It was the local equivalent of a traffic jam. Amy clenched the frame of the vehicle and prayed they would reach the plantation in time.

"Amy, I need to tell you something, too." Her father's eyes stared at the road ahead as he spoke. "As we raced toward Wara, the bridge over the gorge had been damaged by the quake. All of us made it across except Slane before he spotted the damage and warned us. I told him to go back, not to risk it, but he refused. It broke loose as he crossed it and he almost didn't make it. He risked his life for you. Again." He glanced down, shaking his head. "When we reached the village, I had to hold him back to keep him from tearing the glasman limb from limb. Whatever he thought about you lying, he's already forgiven you."

They sped under the sheltering casuarina trees to the helipad where Carlos completed his pre-flight inspection. Slane and Joaquin were saying goodbye to Gloria and started across the lawn toward the helicopter.

Amy jumped out of the Mule and ran to meet them.

"Aw, you came to see me off!" Joaquin teased, throwing his arms wide.

She slowed to a walk, acutely aware of the muddy stains left by her hug from Laila. "Actually, I need to talk to Slane before you go."

Joaquin smiled and hugged her, dropping a kiss on her cheek. "I thought you might." He continued to the chopper and shouted over his shoulder to Slane, "Five minutes! We need to get going if we're going to make it back to the Katie on time."

Suddenly, she stood in front of Slane, and all the apologies she had rehearsed on the ride to Kopi evaporated. She stared at her feet and searched for the words for too many precious seconds before she finally looked up into those dark eyes.

"I need to tell you how sorry I am about lying to my parents and hiding what a hero you are."

He tossed his head and avoided eye contact. "I'm not a hero."

"I told my dad the truth this morning." At that, he met her gaze but remained silent.

"He told me about the bridge. Even after I lied, you were still willing to risk everything for me." Her voice broke. "You are a hero."

He took her hands in his, her smooth pale skin contrasted with his deep tan, marred by various scars on his knuckles and a half-inch scar in the center of the back of his hand. The peculiar location of the scar tickled her memory just as his name had when she first met him.

"*Omlouvám se*. It means 'I'm sorry' in Czech. I'm sorry I have to leave." His gaze cut away toward the mountain. "I have some things I need to do. Things I need to make right. But once I have made it right, I will be back." He squeezed her hands.

And in an instant, the pieces of the puzzle that had eluded her fell into place. His name. His home in Prague. The scar on the back of his hand, just like her online friend from Bolivia had described it—the result of having a microchip removed so the Bolivian drug kingpin could no longer track him.

The stories she'd read on the IMF website played through her mind, rewinding to an alley in Prague, and she jerked her hands away like she'd touched a hot stove.

The look of torment crossed his face again. Pain flashed in his eyes, like the time she caught a glimpse of the healed wounds on his back. The expression vanished as quickly as it appeared. He turned and walked toward the chopper.

Her mind raced through the realization of who he was, who he'd been, and back to who she knew him to be now. All the history melted away as she realized he might be the same person, but he was not the same man he'd been then.

She ran after him and grabbed his arm, spinning him around despite their difference in size. The racket of the helicopter threatened to drown out her words as she shouted, "I know who you are!"

His dark eyes revealed a mixture of relief and fear.

She rushed on. "I've been on this website for missionary kids, and I read about you from one of them. Well, two of them, actually."

"And?" His tone was guarded, steeling himself against rejection.

She hesitated. What could she say? He'd been a bully. A thug. A deserter. A hero.

Joaquin interrupted the moment with a thump on Slane's arm. "It's time to load up. If we don't take off soon, we won't make it back to the Katie in time for our shift."

Slane nodded to his friend and held up one finger before turning back to her. The question in his eyes refused to go unanswered. But the roar of the engine made conversation impossible.

She rose up on her toes and stretched her arms around his neck, pulling his head down quickly, before she had time to reconsider, and planted a kiss on his cheek.

"You've come a long way," she whispered in his ear.

He stood still as a statue as she backed away, the pain in his dark eyes replaced by shock. A grin erased all the angst on his face, but he raised his hand to his ear and shrugged.

He hadn't heard her. He climbed into the seat, and she cupped her hands around her mouth, shouting over the whirr of the helicopter, "You've come a long way!" He smiled and nodded as he pulled the door shut, and she moved back to stand by her father as the chopper lifted off.

One month later

Amy put away the last of the laundry and sank into the chair at the small desk which housed their laptop. She pulled one knee in close to her chest and opened the computer slowly, preparing herself for another disappointment. It had been weeks with no word from Slane or Joaquin, and her hopes for some news lingered on life support. She turned on the computer and her heart jumped at the little number beside the mail icon. One new message. She clicked open the email Joaquin had finally sent her.

Dear Amy,
We made port in Mombasa a few days ago, and I've waited to reach out to you, hoping I would have better news. First, I have to tell you what a huge difference you made in Slane's life. He no longer seemed to be fighting a war with himself. He was excited and seemed to have found a purpose. He said he had to get back to his home and make amends

with some people .

When we arrived in Mombasa, he wanted to go ashore to send a message to someone in Prague. The captain suggested he use the computers at the university library, and he didn't even want to wait until I got off duty to go with him. He said it couldn't wait any longer.

Amy, I hate to have to tell you this way. But Al Shabab attacked the university. They killed at least fifteen people. I searched the hospitals, but they didn't have anyone by his name. They're in the midst of a doctor strike and things are pretty chaotic.

She gasped and had to stop reading as tears blurred the screen. It couldn't be true. Could it? She wiped her eyes and forced herself to read on.

We can't be sure because we didn't find his name on the list of casualties either. I'm so sorry. We've stayed as long in port as we can, but we are setting out tomorrow for our next call.

I've included the picture we took. I wanted you to know you made a difference.

She clicked open the picture of the three of them standing with Laila and her family in front of their newly built home.

After everything, the feeling of satisfaction washed back over her as it had that day, but this time grief marred the picture. She studied the faces staring back, all smiles. All joy and peace. All excited about helping one family rebuild. Whether rebuilding a home or rebuilding a person's life, giving them hope and a future filled her with gratitude. Every tiny act of kindness, trust, generosity, and grace made a difference.

She focused on Slane's image, a grin splitting his face and light shining in his dark eyes. Her finger traced his jaw. How could he be gone? Tears fell again. For all she knew, he died in that library. Or maybe he'd been captured by the Al Shabab. Maybe he had finished at the library before the attack and set off for Prague. She grasped at any possibility except the obvious.

He was not dead. If he'd died in the library, they would have found him. Her heart refused to believe he'd died. But he'd disappeared without a trace. His promise to return once he'd set things right at home teased her with hope.

She wiped her tears and sniffled as she scanned the IMF site for reports from her online friends. She clicked on a message from a short-term missionary in Kenya named Grace. Amy closed her eyes tight and prayed against all odds there would be something posted to give her reason to hope. Grace had posted almost daily about her time in Mombasa working at a local school (and meeting a handsome med student) until a few days ago. About the time Joaquin said the attack had occurred, her account went silent.

Amy pressed her lips into a tight line. She wouldn't give up. Not until she saw absolute proof that Slane was gone. She clicked back to the image Joaquin had shared. If she couldn't search for Slane herself, she'd enlist friends from around the globe to help.

She posted the photo, first with a smiley emoji and a comment about building a house, then with the question, "Have you seen my friend?" She tagged CzechCzick, who had known Slane in Prague, and NotSpiderman, who had escaped the drug cartel with him in Bolivia. Then she sent a private message to

Grace, wondering if that was her real name or another online handle. Maybe Grace knew something about the attack. Maybe she had access to an updated casualty list. It was a long shot, but after all the ways God had shown up for her, she prayed for one more miracle. She thought about Moia, hanging on to hope as she clung to her son's ankle in the sea of mud. Of Miss Maryann praying and flinging the door wide to face her fear. Of Slane, pulling her from the slimy pit. He hadn't given up, and Amy wouldn't give up on him.

The End.

Thank you for coming along on the International Mission Force adventure! The following pages offer several ways for you to continue learning about Papua New Guinea.

First, I've included discussion questions intended to help you process the missionary work and aspects of the culture represented in this story.

Next, I have a glossary of vocabulary words in Tok Pisin, the most common language in Papua New Guinea.

I've also included an appendix with folk stories native to Melanesia and Oceania, the region that includes Papua New Guinea. Unlike in the previous volumes of the International Mission Force series, Papua New Guinea is a country of many diverse cultures rather than a single shared culture. Because of the many different languages and the rugged terrain, tribes do not share a common history or folklore.

Finally, to learn more about Papua New Guinea, I've included a gallery of photos, courtesy of my friend Anton Lutz, and links to articles and blogs on the International Mission Force website at **www.InternationalMissionForce.com**.

If you enjoyed this story, please leave a review on Amazon and Goodreads.com and check out the other titles in this series:

CzechMate

BoliviaKnight

Kenya Quest

You can also follow me on social media at:
Facebook: Felicia Bowen Bridges – Writer
Instagram: Feliciabridges_author
Threads: Feliciabridges_author

Discussion Questions

1. What are the specific ways missionaries serve in Papua New Guinea?

2. Why is Toby drawn to investigate the glasman and to keep it from his parents?

3. What important discovery does Slane make about mankind and about himself?

4. Why is Amy dissatisfied with her life on the mission field in the beginning, and how does she resolve her dissatisfaction?

5. Why does the glasman believe Maryann is to blame for sickness in their tribe?

6. How can missionaries share their faith without destroying cultures or colonizing people groups?

7. What are some examples of how the missionaries in Island Gambit demonstrated respect for the people of PNG?

8. What unique challenges do the residents of PNG face?

9. How did each of the primary characters, Amy, Toby, and Slane, grow in their faith?

10. How does their story encourage you to grow, serve, and live out your faith?

11. Which legends resemble biblical stories of creation?

12. How are these legends similar to the biblical account, and how are they different?

Glossary

bilum - a string bag made by hand in Papua New Guinea. Bags are made by looping or knotless netting or by crocheting. Traditionally, the string used is handmade, normally from plant materials. Bilums are used to carry a wide range of items, from shopping goods in large bilums to personal items in purse-sized varieties. Mothers often carry their babies in bilums.

blauses – brightly colored floral loose-fitting shirts which are common in Papua New Guinea.

boingke – a neck adornment made of horizontal lengths of bamboo which tally the number of pigs owed to the wearer.

casque - hard helmet located between the eyes of a cassowary. It continues to grow with age and is thought to assist in hearing the low, vibrating call of other cassowaries even in the dense jungle environment.

expatriate – a person who lives outside their native country.

gabions – wire cages filled with rocks or concrete to hold steep-sloped landscaping in place.

glasman – native spiritualists found in Papua New Guinea who are believed to see a person's afflictions.

glasmeri – a female counterpart of the glasman.

isthmus – a narrow strip of land with sea on either side, connecting two larger bodies of land.

kaukaus – the Tok Pisin word for a variety of sweet potato grown in Papua New Guinea .

liana - any of various long-stemmed, woody vines that are rooted in the soil at ground level and use trees, as well as other means of vertical support, to climb up to the canopy to get access to well-lit areas of the forest.

liklik house – outhouse.

linguist – a person who studies languages for the purpose of translation.

mumu -traditional dish combining roast pork, kaukau, rice, and greens.

sanguma – a local word meaning sorcery or black magic; belief in sanguma is widespread in the highlands regions of Papua New Guinea.

Tok Pisin - an English-based creole used as a commercial and administrative language in Papua New Guinea.

yambal – a skirt made of woven tree bark, seven layers thick, worn by the Huli tribe.

Appendix: Legends of Melanesia

Kambel Creates the World

In the land where the sun sleeps, he is called Gainjan. The tribes there live in homes high in the treetops to be closer to him. Gainjan created the world, and He alone is almighty. Those who know him well call him by his secret name, a name which must be whispered among those who call themselves His children. It is Kambel.

It is said that Kambel married the great and glorious light, the sun, whose name is Eram. Out of their love was born a child, a beautiful girl named Gufa who carried the light of her mother and the strength of her father. As the daughter of the two great sky dwellers, Gufa cast her light in the darkness of the night sky, but she was all alone.

Kambel, Eram, and beautiful Gufa dwelt in the sky world on an enormous plane suspended above the earth on a rattan cane. At times, Kambel would grow angry with his wife, and they would fight. Gufa would hold tight to the cane as it shook and threatened to snap.

Gufa knew if the cane ever snapped, their world would fall to the ground, all the water of the sky world would fall to the earth and create an enormous deluge. Kambel and Eram and Gufa would be washed away by the massive flood, and all the creatures around them would be drowned, their bodies sucked to the very bottom of the sea. Thus, they knew they must not argue.

One day, long before the time of our people, Kambel grew angry with Eram. Rather than argue and risk the collapse of their world, he chose to climb down to see what the earth contained and whether it would truly be destroyed if the cane snapped due to their quarreling. He slid quickly down the sak'r palm and stood on the earth, gazing at the sky world above and his radiant bride beyond.

He found the earth to be empty of any living thing. There were no people, no animals, not even the bugs that buzz and sting. He was in a dense forest, yet he heard strange noises coming from the tree he had just descended.

He listened intently at the base of the sak'r palm. He knocked on the smooth, black bark, and the sounds increased. Carefully, he swung his stone ax over and over until he felled the tree. The noise continued, and now it sounded very much like voices. He moved slowly down the length of the trunk where it lie on the forest floor.

He split the trunk in half with his stone ax near the top of the tree where the sounds were only confused mumbling, a slight rumble. When the bark split, he jumped back and let out a scream. He could hardly believe his eyes as a whole tribe of people emerged from the black trunk. They were the Gambadi people.

Still Kambel heard noise coming from the trunk of the palm. He listened again, and the sound rose to the hum of the bees during the spring. Quieter and softer than the Gambadi, but clearly coming from the sak'r palm trunk. He swung his razor-sharp stone ax again and split the trunk further. This time, the Semariji tribe emerged, singing as they marched. Kambel marveled at the beauty of their song until the noise from the palm erupted again.

This time the painful howling cried, "Out! Out! Let us out!" Spurred on by their urgent cries, he hacked away at the trunk until it split again. The Tandavi people rose from the trunk, their bodies drenched in dew. They stretched their arms and legs in the sun and flitted about like they were butterflies, intent on seeking a spring blossom.

Only a small section of the tree remained to be split, but Kambel swung his ax again, and the tree split wide with a huge crack. Now the Keraki people emerged, them and their families and their newborn babies. They looked to Kambel and cried, "Father!"

Kambel rejoiced at having brought four tribes out of the trunk of a tree. He desired for all of them to call him father. "You are all my children," he cried. As a good father, he gave each of the tribes their allotted lands.

Kambel wearied of all his work of chopping the tree. He climbed another tree to return to Eram and Gofu and rested until Eram rose the next day. Upon seeing her shine above him, he decided to return to his children, the tribes he had created, and continue his work.

He had so much work left to do to prepare the earth for his children to dwell in! The sky was so close. His children needed more space. The sky world crowded in on the land of his children. They would need clouds and rain, but there was no room for them.

Kambel decided to create all his children needed. He built a bonfire, building up the fire he found at the root of the sak'r palm, the same tree which had given birth to his children. The fire burned brightly, raging strong. He chopped up the woody center of the sago palm, roasting it over the fire until it grew soft.

He formed the soft, roasted nikup into balls and then flattened them out with his hands. When he was satisfied, he hurled them with all his strength toward the sky world. The people called them the sago clouds, and they floated across the sky world and gave shade to the earth below.

Next Kambel formed balls of the nikup and roasted them over his fire until they were hard, like a rock. These he gave to the Bangu people, so they might call down rain from the skies. Still today, the Bangu use the ancient rocks, and through their understanding, cause it to rain.

But still he looked to the sky, and there was not enough space for his people. So, he found a strong rattan cane, even bigger around than his leg, and he braced it under the sky world and pushed with all his might. The cane lifted the sky world up and held it in place, allowing plenty of additional space. With the sky world no longer pressing on the earth, the cool breezes refreshed both Kambel and his creation.

Although the space made him happy, when he looked up to the sky and saw Gofu all alone, he was sad. He gathered tiny pieces of bamboo, which he called kajen, and he heaved them up into the sky to be company for his precious daughter. They glowed with light and became the stars, which always accompany Gofu in the night sky.

Next, Kambel looked at the earth. He knew his children could not survive unless he provided them with food. He dug in the earth and found yams, taro, and coconuts. But Kambel said, "If the coconuts grow in the ground, I cannot see their husks ripen. I cannot know when they are ready to be harvested. So, he took a tall pole, and he used it to attach the coconuts to the top of tall, spindly trees so his children would know when to harvest them.

Kambel sculpted the earth with beautiful towering mountains and narrow canyons. He created rivers to water the land with fresh, clear water and to create lush valleys where all sorts of food would grow. He created the taro, the yam, and the banana plants by hand, and he created all the buzzing things to help the blossoms grow and flourish, and he created fish to swim in the waters and for people to eat.

After all the work he had done, Kambel rested. When he awoke and recalled all the work he had done to create the earth and the animals and mankind, he saw that it was beautiful. It all looked exactly as he had created it at first, but then a strange beast appeared. This was not a beast which Kambel had created, but a monstrous animal with two heads and long, sharp fangs curling down over its jaw. It crawled from under a rock and searched for whom it might devour.

Kambel watched the beast, wondering how it had appeared since it was not part of his creation. Soon other beasts of various kinds appeared, which were not of his creation. Was someone else creating as well? Was the earth itself spawning these monsters? He wasn't sure, but these new creatures spread all over the earth.

It was clear the good things he created were able to change, to morph into different forms, and to create new life. Much of what they created was good, like his original creation, but some was evil.

As he watched, something terribly frightening began to happen. From the hole in the ground where he had chopped down the sak'r palm and where he had gathered the niku he used to form the clouds; a long, black, monstrous serpent slithered out. Its head was giant, and it was called the great Tumbabw'r. Saltwater rushed from the serpent's mouth and as Kambel watched, Tumbabw'r flicked its long, forked tongue and poison flew from his mouth. Whatever it touched withered and died.

Kambel was terrified as he watched the monstrous serpent kill an entire bush filled with berries by spitting a tiny drop of his venom.

What if the venom were spat on his children? Kambel had to stop Tumbabw'r somehow. He strung his bow and aimed his arrows at the monster's face, its heart, its head, but not a single one pierced the thick armor on the creature.

Suddenly the serpent raised up and opened its mouth, breathing the foul stench of death until it overwhelmed Kambel. The monster slithered toward him, and Kambel pulled his strongest spear and brought it down with all his might onto the head of the beast, crushing it in a single blow. The gaping wound gushed saltwater, which tore the wound wider and flooded all Kambel had created. The water swooshed past him and threatened to suck Kambel into the open mouth of the dying leviathan.

Kambel raced to escape the torrent, but he worried that all of his children, his creation, would be wiped out by the flood. He had promised to protect and provide for them, but the water rose faster than he could run. He was out of breath, and his heart was beating so hard it threatened to rip open his chest. The water rose to his knees, his chest, his neck!

He grabbed hold of a loose, heavy branch and began to push back against the flood. He grabbed other branches and slowly pushed and pushed. A few of them snapped, and he grabbed more, determined not to give up against impossible odds. His work now, to save his creation, overwhelmed the effort it had taken to create it.

But at last, the Tumbabw'r drowned. The sea

water it created was its own downfall. Days later, Kambel found the corpse of the serpent on the beach, and he and the elders from each of the tribes he had created worked together to bury the stinking, nasty creature.

Today, in the place where the flood came, there remains a tiny rivulet which runs to the Wassi Kussa River. We remember Kambel, who bravely stopped the floodwaters which would have destroyed all the earth. We admire the beauty of living things, yet we recognize some have arisen which are evil, and we celebrate the creation of Kambel as we hear the song of the Semariji, just as it was when they emerged from the sak'r palm, a melodious tribute to the day they were born and the one who created them.

The Two Jealous Brothers

Amongst the Arapesh and along the north coast of Papua New Guinea, the story is told of two brothers who were orphaned. They lived in the woods and worked the garden their parents had started, but they were all alone.

One day, the older brother said to the younger, "I will go fish and bring them back for us to eat." So, he set out in his canoe and gathered many fish. But when darkness came, he was too far from home. He saw a fire burning on the opposite bank of the river and rowed the canoe toward the campfire.

An old crone sat by the fire and greeted him. She asked about him, and he told her how he had lost his parents and had gone fishing so he and his brother might survive. She told him to sleep by the fire and not to open his eyes until morning because the young women were coming to dance by the fire.

He obeyed her and when he set out in the morning to return to his brother, she gifted him a mango. "You must keep the mango with you and row toward home. As you row, it will become a young woman for you."

The older brother put the mango in his canoe and rowed toward the other shore. Just before they reached the edge, the mango transformed into a beautiful young woman, as lovely as a blossom. He brought her ashore and introduced her to his younger brother.

But his brother became angry and jealous over the woman, and the two brothers fought. When the older brother slept that night, his younger brother came with a post and killed him and took the woman for himself.

The Mekeo Legend of the Two Brothers

In the Central Province, the Mekeo tribe tells the story of two brothers who resemble the first biblical siblings. According to the tale, one brother could only eat fruit and the other only ate meat.

Like Cain, the vegetarian brother became jealous of his brother, so he followed his sibling to see how he was getting so much meat. He saw his brother pause beside a large hill and speak some strange words. The hill opened upon his command, and the brother emerged a short time later with a wallaby and two scrub hens.

In his jealousy, the brother decided to imitate his sibling. He approached the hill and spoke the words he'd heard his brother speak, but when the hill opened up, he was too slow, and all the animals escaped.

His brother became angry because the animals were all gone, and they began to fight. But fearing they would kill one another, their wise wives found a way to resolve their dispute. They each told their husband about a terrible ogre who was threatening their lives and the lives of their children, and they sent them to fight the ogre instead.

The Keraki Tribe and the Gaining

On the southwest coast of Papua New Guinea, the Keraki tribe recalls that long ago the first sky beings came to earth from their sky world. They were called Gaining.

They came for a time and stayed among the people, but when their time on the earth ended, they returned to the sky—all except two. Bugal the snake and Warger the crocodile remained on the earth and hid in the bush.

Whenever the heavy rains come, the Keraki know the sky beings are angry and displeased. Many fear one day the great rattan cane, which is the only thing holding the sky world in place, may break. And so, when the rains come, they stand guard with their weapons in hand, lest any of the sky beings fall from their world.

The Ayon Legend of Tumbreniuk

Among the Ayon tribe, the story is told of Tumbreniuk, who once dwelt in the sky world. Tumbreniuk often climbed down from the sky to the earth in order to hunt and fish.

One day, when Tumbreniuk prepared to return with his bounty, he found the rope had been cut, and he could not return to the sky world. He cried out, and when his wife looked down and saw him, she realized he could not return and also cried.

She threw down fire and fruits and vegetables of every kind in order to help her husband. She also threw down four cucumbers. When the man went to gather the fruits and vegetables, he discovered the cucumbers had transformed into four women.

When he returned, he found the women had completed all his work, and he heard the women laughing.

All the villages of the Ayon tribe are descended from Tumbreiuk and his four wives.

The Spider's Lesson

Once there was a spider who carefully wove a delicate web near the edge of the village. The spider worked hard and constructed her web so it would catch the insects she needed for food. Finally, after much hard work, her nest was done, and the real waiting began!

She waited every day for some insect to fly into her web. Finally, a butterfly flew into her web, but before she could get to it, it tore the web apart and flew away. The spider did not give up. She worked hard every day to rebuild her web, and finally she finished it once again. She waited patiently for another insect to fly into her web.

Eventually, a dragonfly flew into her web. She scurried over to it and injected it with poison and began to wrap it in her web. But the dragonfly fell to the ground and ants carried it away.

Still the spider did not give up hope. She worked very hard every day to repair her web once again. When she finished, she waited patiently for another insect. Sure enough, a moth flew into her web, and she captured it and ate it, rejoicing at her good fortune.

The moral of the story is we must be patient and then we will enjoy the fruit of our hard work.

The Trobriand Islanders Origin Story

In the Milne Bay Province, on the northern side of the island, near Massim, there are a number of tribes which share an origin story quite different from the lore of other regions.

According to their oral history, life existed below ground long before it came to the surface. This life below was exactly like their life now because those who emerged from the ground brought with them their customs and rules for conduct, as well as all of their understanding, their skills, and their magic.

The Trobriand islanders are a clan among whom each sub-clan has a specific location and tradition regarding who and where their family first came above ground. This particular rock, or lump of coral, or grove is associated with their family and their ancestor claimed it for their family.

The islanders revered one particular site on the peninsula of Kirawina as where the first creatures to emerge from the earth came forth. These creatures were the iguana, the dog, the pig, and the snake. These four creatures became the animal ancestors of the four primary clans.

The Legend of Ipila's Creation

Near the Binaturi River, the story is told that Ipila created the first man by carving him from a piece of wood. When Ipila formed the man, he painted his face with sago mixed with water, which miraculously brought him to life. His eyes were the first to open, and then his nostrils quivered, and he roared like a crocodile.

Ipila named the man Nugu. Nugu asked Ipila to make three more men as companions. But once Ipila had created them, they refused to learn and obey Ipila's teaching. They turned their back and rejected Ipila. Two of them were no longer satisfied with eating sago and began to kill animals for food.

As soon as they had eaten the animals, they turned into half-crocodiles. All the other creations, Nugu, the other man, and even the animals, did not want anything to do with the half-crocodile men.

The half-crocodile men wanted to create companions, too, but they found they could only create men because Ipila secretly thwarted their efforts.

All those who claim the crocodile as their father are descended from these two men.

Now, Ipila became angry with Nugu for creating the half-crocodiles, and so he condemned Nugu to carry the whole world upon his shoulders for eternity.

This is why the people of this tribe know only what they know. They do not know why they are alive or what is happening beyond their part of the world.

The Legend of Towjatuwa

There was once a man named Towjatuwa who had a wife, and his wife was about to give birth. When the time came and he sent for the midwife, the midwife told him he must get a sharp rock, because the baby could not be born in the ordinary way. The midwife would need to operate on his wife in order to deliver the baby.

She sent him down to the Tami river to find a sharp rock, but while he looked for the rock, he heard a voice. He turned to greet the stranger only to find it was a large crocodile with shining, sharp teeth. He started to run away, but the crocodile spoke again, saying, "I am Watuwe. What are you searching for in the river?"

Towjatuwa told Watuwe his story, and the giant crocodile agree to help the man's wife deliver the baby. Sure enough, the crocodile helped the woman deliver a healthy baby boy, whom they named Narrowa.

"Now I ask one thing," said the crocodile. "One day, Narrowa will grow to be a great hunter, but you must teach him it is forbidden for him to hunt or eat the crocodile because I have saved his life." Towjatuwa agreed, and ever since, his descendants have lived on the Tami river and protected the crocodiles.

The moral of the story is we should repay the kindness done to us. If we cannot return life for life, we must at least remember the kindness and honor it.

Legend of How Two Tribes were Separated

On the Northern Coast of Papua New Guinea, there is a story that long ago there lived a woman who was not married but had a daughter. Her daughter died, and the woman carried her from town to town until she found a village where she might bury her daughter. She came to the village of Tangu, and the men of the village allowed her to bury her daughter.

One of the men of the village, the younger of two brothers, then took the woman as his wife, and she gave birth to two sons.

One day when visiting the grave of her daughter, she discovered a pool of saltwater flowing from the grave with fish swimming in it. She caught a fish and took it and some of the water to her family. The water and fish had a miraculous effect on her sons—they grew overnight to be men!

Her husband's older brother became jealous when he saw how her sons had grown. She told him about the pool, and he went to the grave, but instead of taking a fish, he caught a large eel. As soon as he caught it, the ground quaked and water burst forth from the ground, separating the man from his village and his brother.

After a long time, the brothers exchanged messages on leaves cast on the waters. It soon became clear the one brother could not achieve anything on his own but could only copy what his brother had done.

The Legend of Maruwai

Once there was a man named Maruwai. He was very strong and was a good hunter. He used a bow and arrow made from cassowary bone to hunt wild pigs. The day came when a great drought threatened the village where he lived. He wanted to leave the village and find water, and his parents agreed to let him go.

No matter how far he went, though, he could not find any water or any rain. He asked his neighbor, Bodofon, to help him. His friend gave him a special bowl called Upih bowl, which is made from leaves of the Areca tree. The magical bowl would collect water wherever he placed it. But Bodofon warned Maruwai, "You must promise not to leave the bowl carelessly about. You must guard it carefully."

As Maruwai returned home, he saw a huge, wild boar, and he set the bowl down on the ground in order to hunt the pig. He could think of nothing else but that his family needed food because of the drought, and this boar would feed them well.

When he returned, the water the bowl collected had become a river! This river is still named for Maruwai today.

The lesson of Maruwai's story is we must do what we have promised in order to have success in life in the future.

The Legend of Takaro

Long ago, when the islands had only recently been fished up from the sea, and before the French and British divided the island nation of Vanuatu into colonies, Takaro created mankind.

Takaro soaked in the mud created by the hot springs on the island. From the thick, black ooze, he shaped the figure of a man. And then another. And another. Ten lifeless forms lying on the bank. Takaro leaned over the first one and released his breath over eyes which blinked in response, over ears which turned toward the faint sound of the air rushing from his lips. He exhaled over the hands which flexed in response and over legs which bent to rise up from the ground. Takaro surveyed his creations, each of the ten a perfect specimen.

Yet he wasn't satisfied.

"Come, light a fire. Prepare some food." He commanded his creations, and they obeyed.

When they had finished, he lined them up like pawns on a chessboard. He studied each one carefully before choosing his mark. He hefted a piece of ripe fruit in one hand. He aimed with deadly precision and threw the fruit at one of his creations, and the fruit burst open when it hit its target. The juice and pulp streamed down over the mud, and even as it did, the form's shape evolved. Curves arose and hollows formed. Features softened and muscles relaxed.

Takaro spoke to the woman he'd created. "Go inside and wait. As I send these in to you, decide who they each shall be to you." With that, Takaro ushered his new creations, on-by-one before his crowning achievement.

As the first entered the hut, Takaro whispered, "Ask the woman for fire!" The man asked, and the woman greeted him as her older brother. The second approached and Takaro told him, "Ask the woman for water." The man asked, and she rewarded him by calling him her youngest brother. One by one, she resolved each of the questions and she greeted each one as a family member.

Only when she reached the final man did she refer to him as husband. Takaro placed her hand on the man's hand and then put the man's other hand in his place on top. "You have been joined together. Therefore, you must revere the wisdom of your God in bringing you together and promise to remain only to one another forever."

FAITH IS HER ONLY DEFENSE
INTERNATIONAL MISSION FORCE SERIES
CZECHMATE
FELICIA BRIDGES
THE GREATEST ENEMY LIES WITHIN
INTERNATIONAL MISSION FORCE SERIES
BOLIVIAKNIGHT
FELICIA BRIDGES
FEAR HELD HER CAPTIVE,
BUT FAITH SET HER FREE
INTERNATIONAL MISSION FORCE SERIES
KENYAQUEST
FELICIA BRIDGES

INTERNATIONAL
MISSION FORCE

About the Author

Felicia Bridges' nomadic childhood as an Army BRAT created a passion for missions and travel which leads her writing on many an adventure. Her first foray into fiction is the award-winning International Mission Force series which tells the tales of teenage missionaries around the world who connect online. Her bachelor's degree in psychology, two decades' experience as an HR manager, thirty years' parenting four children, and twenty years as a pastor's wife add up to lots of humorous insights into human behavior. Felicia is happiest sharing funny stories with a stranger in line at the grocery store or an auditorium full of people.

You can find out more about the International Mission Force at
www.InternationalMissionForce.com - come join our community!
I'm on Facebook at Felicia Bowen Bridges – Writer and Instagram @feliciabridges_author.

To start your adventure, ask about the International Mission Force series wherever you find your favorite books.